Which elements of the front cover did the artist pick up for the kaleidoscope?

Can you find the fish in the design to the left?

Sourcebook
Volume 1

Program Authors

Linda Hoyt

Michael Opitz

Robert Marzano

Sharon Hill

Yvonne Freeman

David Freeman

Rigby

A Harcourt Achieve Imprint

www.Rigby.com

1-800-531-5015

Welcome to Literacy by Design,
Where Reading Is...

Discovering

Imagining

Questioning

Literacy by Design: Sourcebook Volume 1
Grade 4

ISBN-13:   978-1-4189-4038-6
ISBN-10:   1-4189-4038-0

Printed in China
1 2 3 4 5 6 7 8   985 13 12 11 10 09 08 07 06

Thinking

Exploring

American Journeys

THEME 1 American Dreams Pages 4–33

Modeled Reading

Historical Fiction Oranges on Golden Mountain
by Elizabeth Partridge 6

Vocabulary
ambition, gleaming, flourished, ancestor, artifact.....................8

Comprehension Strategy !
Make Connections 10

Shared Reading

Interview Two Homes by Alice McGinty.....................12

Word Study
Short Vowels Review 14

Interactive Reading

Realistic Fiction The Mystery of the Box in the Wall
by Tisha Hamilton 16

Vocabulary
cautious, settler, prosper, immigrant, youth 22

Poem "Working on the Transcontinental Railroad"
by Ruth Siburt 24

Word Study
Initial Consonants Review 26

Biography Sam Goldwyn, Picture This. . . .
by Erica Lauf 28

THEME ② A Place for Us Pages 34–63

Modeled Reading

Expository Coming to America: The Story of Immigration by Betsy Maestro 36

Vocabulary
permanent, relocation, origin, regulate, necessities............... 38

Comprehension Strategy !
Determine Importance 40

Shared Reading

Historical Fiction Family Treasures by Jerrill Parham 42

Word Study
Consonant Blends *sn-* and *-st* 44

Interactive Reading

Expository The World on Your Plate by Neil Fairbairn 46

Vocabulary
belief, border, accompany, audience, nationality..................... 52

Poem "Celebrating Our Roots" by Abby Jones 54

Word Study
Word Families 56

Play The Fair by Sue Miller 58

THEME ③ **So Many Kinds of Animals** Pages 66–95

Modeled Reading

Mystery Seal by Judy Allen 68

Vocabulary
variety, species, researchers, abandon, definite 70

Comprehension Strategy !
Infer..72

Shared Reading

Expository Weird Animals by Ann Weil................................74

Word Study
Long Vowels 76

Interactive Reading

Humor Slimy, Spiny Riddles by Alice Leonhardt.................78

Vocabulary
characteristic, identify, categorize,
invertebrate, vertebrate 84

Poem "Vertebrate, or Invertebrate—What's my ID?"
by Ruth Siburt...86

Grammar
Nouns..88

Encyclopedia Animals by Renée Carver 90

THEME ④ **Seeds, Fruits, and Flowers** Pages 96–125

Modeled Reading

Memoir Century Farm: 100 Years on a Family Farm
by Cris Peterson...98

Vocabulary
require, pollinate, equipment, reproduction, century............ 100

Comprehension Strategy !
Create Images..102

Shared Reading

Realistic Fiction Mrs. McClary's Very Weird Garden
by David Dreier 104

Grammar
Proper Nouns..106

Interactive Reading

Observation Log Waking Up a Bean by Darlene Stille 108

Vocabulary
criteria, conditions, germinate, cones, adapt 114

Poem "Ode to the Giant Redwood" by Tisha Hamilton 116

Word Study
Reference Materials.. 118

Fairy Tale The Pea Blossom
retold by Ernestine Geisecke 120

Across the U.S.A.

THEME ⑤ One Country, Many Regions
Pages 128–157

Modeled Reading

Adventure Fire Storm by Jean Craighead George.................130

Vocabulary
canyon, region, surround, solution, dense 132

Comprehension Strategy
Use Fix-Up Strategies...134

Shared Reading

Personal Narrative The Superstition Mountains
by Bradley Hannan...136

Word Study
Synonyms and Antonyms 138

Interactive Reading

Fantasy Who Believes in Buried Treasure?
by Jeanie Stewart 140

Vocabulary
aspect, impact, alter, climate, plateau...............................146

Song "This Land Is Your Land" by Woodie Guthrie................148

Word Study
Multiple-Meaning Words 150

Expository Take a Virtual Trip by Alice McGinty.................152

THEME ⑥ The Land Shapes People's Lives
Pages 158–187

Modeled Reading

Observation Log Arctic Lights, Arctic Nights
by Debbie S. Miller 160

Vocabulary
farmland, fertile, vast, horizon, reflection 162

Comprehension Strategy ❗
Synthesize 164

Shared Reading

Realistic Fiction My A-Mazing Summer Vacation
by Myka-Lynne Sokoloff 166

Word Study
Homonyms...168

Interactive Reading

Memoir The Gigantic Redwoods: A Memoir by Mrs. J. B.
Rideout retold by M. J. Cosson 170

Vocabulary
access, surroundings, recreation, port, altitude......................176

Photo Essay Key West, Florida by Sue Miller......................178

Grammar
Verbs 180

Historical Fiction Mountain Homestead
by Linda Lott...182

ix

THEME ⑦ **Why Does Water Move?** Pages 190–219

Modeled Reading

Realistic Fiction Very Last First Time
by Jan Andrews 192

Vocabulary
visible, tide, shore, chisel, wedge.................................194

Comprehension Strategy !
Monitor Understanding 196

Shared Reading

Procedural Making Waves by Katie Sharp............................198

Grammar
Helping Verbs.. 200

Interactive Reading

Adventure Typhoon! by John Manos.................................202

Vocabulary
swift, analyze, model, current, coastline............................ 208

Poem "The Vessel" by M. J. Cosson 210

Word Study
Inflected Endings -ed, -ing, and -s..................................212

Persuasive Essay Fighting Coastal Erosion:
Why We Should Save Our Coastal Wetlands
by Mary Dylewski 214

THEME 8 What Makes Soil Different? Pages 220–249

Modeled Reading

Expository The Living Earth by Eleonore Schmid...............222

Vocabulary
consist, geology, property, layer, artificial............................ 224

Comprehension Strategy !
Ask Questions 226

Shared Reading

Fantasy A Very Dirty Subject by Karen Lowther 228

Grammar
Adjectives 230

Interactive Reading

Personal Narrative The Case of Vanishing Soil
by Darlene Stille.. 232

Vocabulary
combine, separate, replace, texture, particles 238

Poem "What Does Weather Do to Soil?" by Ann Weil.... 240

Word Study
Prefix un- 242

Realistic Fiction The Black Blizzard
by Jo Zarboulas 244

1

Just off the Ship (Ellis Island), 1922
Martha Walter (1875–1976)

THEME **1** **American Dreams**

THEME **2** **A Place for Us**

Viewing

The artist who painted this picture was Martha Walter. She painted a series of pictures about immigrants who traveled by ship to Ellis Island, in New York City. This picture shows families who have arrived from Eastern Europe in search of a new life in America.

1. The artist painted this picture more than seventy-five years ago. What clues can you find in the picture that let you know this is not a present-day painting?

2. What details does Walter show us about this scene at Ellis Island in 1922?

3. If Walter painted an immigration scene today, what changes do you think she would make? What part of the artist's painting might stay the same?

In This UNIT

In this unit, you will read about why people immigrated to the United States and how they settled in different areas of the country. You will also read about the many cultures that make up the United States.

Contents

American Dreams

Modeled Reading

Historical Fiction Oranges on Golden Mountain
by Elizabeth Partridge 6

Vocabulary
ambition, gleaming, flourished, ancestor, artifact.....................8

Comprehension Strategy
Make Connections 10

Shared Reading

Interview Two Homes by Alice McGinty 12

Word Study
Short Vowels Review 15

Interactive Reading

Realistic Fiction The Mystery of the Box in the Wall
by Tisha Hamilton 16

Vocabulary
cautious, youth, immigrant, prosper, settler 22

Poem "Working on the Transcontinental
Railroad, 1869" by Ruth Siburt 24

Word Study
Initial Consonants Review 26

Biography Samuel Goldwyn, Picture This . . .
by Erica Lauf..28

Oranges on Golden Mountain

by

Elizabeth Partridge

illustrated by

AKI SOGABE

Precise Listening

Precise listening is listening for details. Listen to the focus questions your teacher will read to you.

Chinese Fishing Villages

Quite a Catch!

Many Chinese immigrants settled in fishing villages along the coast of northern California. The villagers fished for the shrimp that **flourished** in the bays. But, in those days, few people in the United States ate shrimp. So the villagers dried most of their catch and sold it in China. Eventually, though, people in the United States developed a taste for **gleaming** shrimp. Today, it is very popular.

Fun Fact!

The first Chinese who came to California did not come for shrimp. Most came for gold! Each had the **ambition** to strike it rich in the Gold Rush.

CHINA CAMP State Park

China Camp was one of the largest fishing villages. The village is now part of China Camp State Park. Visit the park and see what life was like in an earlier time. Each building, photograph, and **artifact** can tell us something about the way people lived in the past.

Fun Fact!

Frank Quan still fishes for shrimp from China Camp. His **ancestor** was one of the village's early settlers.

Structured Vocabulary Discussion

When your teacher says a vocabulary word, write all of the words the vocabulary word makes you think of. When your teacher says, "Stop," share your words with a partner. Take turns explaining to each other why the words on your list popped into your mind.

Throughout the week, add to your vocabulary journal entries. Record new insights and other words that relate to this week's vocabulary.

Picture It

Draw a chart like this in your vocabulary journal. Write in the circles things that are **gleaming**.

silver

gleaming

Copy this chart in your vocabulary journal. What kind of thing could be an **artifact**?

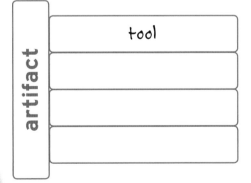

artifact	tool

Make Connections

Try to make connections between what you read to what you already know. Thinking about what you have heard or seen or done or read before will help you learn more from what you read.

A **CONNECTION** is a link between two ideas.

To make a connection, relate your reading to what you already know.

TURN AND TALK Listen as your teacher reads from *Oranges on Golden Mountain*. The people and events may remind you of something you have heard, seen, done, or read before. With a partner, discuss the connections you can make to something you already know.

- Think about how Jo Lee is feeling. Have you ever felt this way?
- Have you read about other people who faced similar situations?

"It's been three years since your father died," his mother told Jo Lee. "All that time I've kept these coins. Now we must use them. I will send you to fish with Fourth Uncle on Golden Mountain." Her mouth trembled, holding her sorrow inside. "At least in the fishing village your belly will always be full."

"I won't go!" Jo Lee cried out. "I don't mind a little hunger!" He threw himself on his mother, wrapping his arms tight around her neck. "I don't even know Fourth Uncle."

TAKE IT WITH YOU Making connections helps you link what you already know with what is new in the text. As you read other selections, try to make connections to things you have heard, seen, done, or read before. Use a chart like the one below to help you make connections.

In the Text	This Reminds Me Of...
Jo Lee's mother is sending Jo Lee to California to live with his uncle. Jo Lee doesn't know anything about his uncle.	The first time I went to camp, I was scared. I didn't have any friends going with me. I didn't know what to expect.
Because Jo Lee is going so far away from his family, he is afraid and sad to leave his mother.	I read a story once about a girl who came to America for the first time. She was scared, too.

Two Homes

by Alice McGinty

Have you ever wondered what it would be like to grow up in a home where things come in twos? Two cultures, two languages, two kinds of food. Reshma Shah knows. She grew up this way. She is an Indian American. Her parents moved to the United States from India before she was born. Reshma remembers many things about her childhood.

Why did your parents come to America?

"My father was a good student. He came to America to continue his college education—to get his master's degree—and decided to stay. He had arranged to marry my mother in India. Instead, he asked her to come to America, too."

Your parents were immigrants. How did that affect you?

"My parents felt that as immigrants they had to work hard. We all had to prove ourselves. I often felt like I had to do well for my family. I had to do well as an Indian."

How were Indian and American cultures part of your life?

"We spoke Gujarati—our Indian language—at home. We were also strict vegetarians. Still, we ate Indian food during the week and American food on the weekends.

Did your two cultures ever clash or lead to problems?

"I was sent to boarding school in India when I was 13. My parents felt that I needed to learn more about my Indian heritage. Going there, I felt a culture shock. In America, I looked different from everyone. Still, I felt American. In India, I looked just like everyone, but I felt very different. Those two years were hard, but they opened my eyes to the Indian people. I understood them. I loved the music. I loved the dance. I loved the food."

Did you like growing up as an Indian in America?

"Yes. My parents have a great attitude about our Indian heritage. It is, 'We are proud of who we are.'"

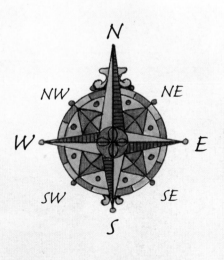

A Taste of India

Indian food is among the finest in the world. It ranges from mild to very spicy. The Taste of India Restaurant serves dishes from many regions of India. Thanks for being our guest. Enjoy your meal!

Soups and Salads
Spicy Indian Soup

Tomato and Cucumber Salad

Chicken and Duck Dishes
Pepper Chicken

Yogurt Chicken

Duck Surprise

Lamb and Pork Dishes
Lamb Curry

Curried Pork

Seafood Dishes
Spicy Fried Fish

Shrimp Grill

Vegetarian Dishes
Egg Curry

Mock Duck

Desserts
Carrot Pudding

Cheese Balls in Sweet Milk

Short Vowels Review

Activity One

About Short Vowels

The letters *a, e, i, o,* and *u* are vowels. Some vowels make a short sound, like the *a* in *hat* or the *o* in *hot*. As your teacher reads the menu from *A Taste of India*, listen for the short-vowel sounds. Keep in mind that some words may include other vowels in addition to short vowels.

Short Vowels in Context

With a partner, read the menu. Write each short-vowel word you find in a chart like the one below. Underline the short vowel and say the word aloud. Then think of another word with the same short-vowel sound.

WORD	VOWEL	WORD WITH THE SAME VOWEL SOUND
egg	e	went

Activity Two

Explore Words Together

tan	pet
big	mist
rug	rib

The list on the right contains words with a short-vowel sound. Change each word to another short-vowel word by changing the vowel. For example, change the *a* in the word *tan* to an *e* and make the word *ten*. Talk with your partner about your list of old and new short-vowel words.

Activity Three

Explore Words in Writing

Choose three of the new words you made in the last activity. Write a sentence that uses each word and one additional word with the same consonants, but different short vowel.

The Mystery of the Box in the Wall

by Tisha Hamilton

The Kahlos loved their new house in Texas, but everyone missed the wide windows of their old house in Mexico. That's why Mama and Papa were knocking holes in the walls. They were going to put in big new windows.

When they found the mysterious box, they did not stop working to look at it. Instead Papa called, "Elena! Miguel! Come see what we found." The children came running. He handed them a dusty metal box. "It was hidden inside this wall," Papa explained, "like buried treasure. Miguel, see if you can get it open."

Elena was 9 years old, and her brother Miguel was 11. Their eyes grew wide and excited as they examined the box. Miguel undid the clasp, cautious not to break it. What would they find inside?

The hinges squeaked and groaned as Miguel and Elena tried to pry the box open. Finally the lid swung back. Elena and Miguel found a stack of old papers and faded brown photographs.

Have you ever heard of a box hidden in a wall?

A collection of old letters was tied with ribbon. They began to sort through them, but they had trouble reading the old-fashioned handwriting.

It wasn't the handwriting itself that caused the problem. It was the language it was written in. Some words they recognized as slightly different spellings of Spanish words. Other words, though, didn't seem to match any of the languages they knew.

Have you ever seen something written in another language? When?

"Mama and Papa, how old is this house?" Miguel asked.

"The realtor told us it is almost one hundred years old," Mama remembered.

"That's right," Papa agreed. "It was built in the early 1900s."

"Did people speak different Spanish then?" Elena asked.

"Here, let me see," Mama offered. Miguel handed her a faded photograph with some of the strange writing on the back. "I can see why you might think this is Spanish," she told the children. "It's similar, but I think it's Italian."

"Who speaks Italian?" Elena wondered.

"Italians," her father said, laughing. "From Italy," he added.

"It's like we are from Mexico and we speak Spanish," Miguel exclaimed. "Maybe the people who lived here were like us. Maybe they came from another country to make a new life in America."

Say Something Technique
Take turns reading a section of text, covering it up, and then saying something about it to your partner. You may say any thought or idea that the text brings to your mind.

"The people we bought this house from did have an Italian last name," Mama recalled.

"Maybe this box belonged to them," Elena suggested. "Maybe we should give it back."

"How could we find them?" Miguel wanted to know.

"Perhaps the realtor can tell us," Mama put in. "Her business card is on the refrigerator."

Elena read the phone number off the business card while her mother tapped the numbers on the phone. When Mrs. Flores answered, Mrs. Kahlo explained the problem. The realtor promised to help.

Mrs. Flores got in touch with the Batalis, who had sold the house. It wasn't long before both families sat down together under the same roof, where the Batalis used to live and the Kahlos lived now.

Mrs. Batali carried a gurgling baby. Mr. Batali carried a briefcase. Two older children, a boy and a girl about the same age as Miguel and Elena, smiled shyly.

Have you ever moved into a new house?

"I can't tell you how grateful I am," Mr. Batali began. Then he opened his briefcase and took out some old papers. "My great-grandfather built this house," he explained. "My grandfather found these in a drawer after his father died." When he held up the papers, Elena gasped.

"The writing!" she exclaimed. "It's the same."

"Yes," Mr. Batali agreed. "This box solves a great family mystery. My great-grandfather wrote a letter." He unfolded a page from his briefcase and read, "It is important to discover the past, so I have hidden it in this house."

"What does that mean?" Miguel asked.

"That's what we always wondered, too," Mr. Batali told him. "We didn't understand what he meant, and even though we searched and searched, we never found anything in the house to answer our question. I think this box holds the secret."

How do you feel when you find something you have lost?

He began poring over the old documents. Then he laughed. "My great-grandfather was ahead of his time," he told them. "Way back in 1908 he created a time capsule! It's like he actually wanted to leave a record of his time for future generations."

Mr. Batali explained that everything in the box told the story of what his family's life was like a hundred years ago. Some of the old photos were pictures of the family they left in Italy when they came to America. Other photos showed what the land looked like before the house was built. Finally, there was a journal in which the great-grandfather told of the struggles of beginning life in a new country. Mr. Batali smiled as he thumbed through the pages. "My great-grandfather worked hard. He was eventually able to prosper. He was very proud of that."

That gave Elena an idea. After the Batalis left, she shared it with her family. "We could make our own time capsule," she explained. "Before we put in the new windows, we could put our time capsule inside the wall."

What would you put in a time capsule?

The Kahlos had lots of fun finding things to put in their family time capsule. They included photos of their home in Mexico, a peso, a colorful woven belt that Elena had outgrown, and other things as well. Before they sealed the box, the members of the family wrote down some memories of their lives before and after they moved. The box is there still, waiting for one of Elena's or Miguel's grandchildren to discover a surprise from the past.

Think and Respond

Reflect and Write

- You and your partner have read *The Mystery of the Box in the Wall*. Discuss the connections you made.

- Choose three connections that you made. Write them on three index cards. Share them with another partner pair.

Short Vowels in Context

Reread *The Mystery of the Box in the Wall* and find the words that contain short vowel sounds. Have a contest with a partner to see who can find the most words.

Turn and Talk

MAKE CONNECTIONS

Discuss with a partner what you have learned so far about making connections.

- How do you make a connection?

- How does making connections help you learn more from what you read?

Choose one connection you made. Explain that connection to a partner. Use details to explain your thinking.

Critical Thinking

Talk about what it must have been like for the Kahlos and Mr. Batali's great-grandparents to move to a new country. Choose one of the two families, either the Kahlos or the Batalis. Write the name of the family on a piece of paper. Next, write at least five words to describe feelings that family might have had when they first came to the United States.

Finally, answer these questions.

- Which of these words also applied to the family you did not write about?

- What other words can you think of that might apply better to that family? Explain your opinions.

Life in a New Country

Hi, Carlos,

Guess what my parents found when they tore down a wall in our house? A sealed box! Papa gave it to me to open. I was very **cautious**—I had no idea what might be inside.

I found a bunch of old letters and photos of an **immigrant** family! I couldn't read the letters—they were in Italian.

We found the people's great-grandson—Mr. Batali. He and his family came for the box. He's a lawyer. Papa says that it proves you can **prosper** in the United States if you work hard.

Mr. Batali said that his great-grandparents came from Italy in the 1890s. Wow, it must have been tough to be a **settler** in Texas then. He told us that his great-grandparents were very poor when they got here. It reminded me of what I learned in school about Chinese immigrants.

I wonder what stories my great-grandchildren will tell about my **youth** in this new country. Write me!

Miguel

Structured Vocabulary Discussion

Work with a partner to complete the following sentences about your vocabulary words.

Immigrant and **settler** are *similar* because they both . . .

Cautious and **youth** are *different* because . . .

Throughout the week, add to your vocabulary journal entries. Record new insights and other words that relate to this week's vocabulary.

Picture It

Draw charts like these two in your vocabulary journal. Give three examples of being **cautious**.

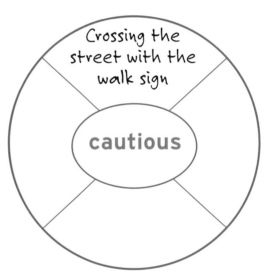

Crossing the street with the walk sign

cautious

Fill in the boxes with things that will help you **prosper**.

prosper
good food

WORKING ON THE TRANSCONTINENTAL RAILROAD, 1869

by Ruth Siburt

Paddy O'Toole

In Ireland, I grew potatoes, pure
Enough to feed my country—sure
And then the blight we couldn't cure
Left them rotting, rank and foul
—but that was years ago.

In America, I bossed a gang
Of Irish youth; their picks did clang.
Laying rails, our hammers rang
'Cross the mountains, sands, and flats
Pushing forward, never back
—always forward, never back.

Li Chen

In China, I lived on the street
Until I sailed across the sea.
I dreamed I'd be rich at twenty-three.
Half my pay the captain owns
—and I have years to go.

In America, I swung pick and ax
Laying miles and miles of tracks.
I ate my fill and broke my back
Building ties from west to east
Pushing forward, never back
—always forward, never back.

A Visit to Ellis Island

Dear Christine,

New York City is great! The city is so huge! It makes Minneapolis seem really, really small.

When we got here, my brother and father wanted to go to a baseball game. But my mother and I wanted to see the city. So we split up for the day. The guys went to a Yankees game, and Mom and I saw the sights.

We toured the Statue of Liberty. That was awesome! She really is green—the statue, not my mom! Then we went to Ellis Island. It's the place where immigrants used to have to stop when they came to the United States. I wasn't that interested in going there until Mom told me that my great-great-grandparents came through there in 1906 when they left Russia.

I learned that lots of Russian Jews like my great-great-grandparents came through Ellis Island. They were trying to escape bad treatment by the Russian government. The place really made me want to know more about my family and that period of history.

Hugs,

Sarah

Initial Consonants Review

Activity One

About Initial Consonants

All the letters of the alphabet except vowels are consonants. Many words begin with consonants. The *g* in *gate* is an example of an initial consonant. As your teacher reads Sarah's letter, listen carefully for *g, m, p, f, r,* and *s* at the beginning of words.

Initial Consonants in Context

With a partner, make a list of the words in Sarah's letter that begin with *g, m, p, f, r,* or *s*. Next, pick one word from your list for each consonant. Write the meaning of each word that you picked.

Activity Two

Explore Words Together

cake	kind
lad	lint
bet	hole

Look at the words to the right. Work with a partner to see how many words you can make by replacing the initial consonant with *g, m, p, f, r,* or *s*. For example, by replacing the first letter *c* in the word *cake* with other consonants, you can make the words *make, fake,* and *rake*.

Activity Three

Explore Words in Writing

Write a short description of your school. In each sentence, include at least three words beginning with *g, m, p, f, r,* or *s*. Here is an example: "Our school is a great place to learn more about reading." Share your description with a partner.

SAMUEL GOLDWYN

Picture This . . .

by Erica Lauf

When Schmuel Gelbfisz was born, no one could have guessed his future. Later known as Samuel Goldwyn, he would make movies that captured the dreams of people everywhere. But first he had to travel halfway around the world to make his own dreams come true. His life story would make a great movie.

Scene One . . .

1895. A crowded street on the edge of Warsaw. A thin, ragged boy trudges down the road, away from the city. He turns and takes one last look back.

Schmuel was born in 1879 in the Jewish part of Warsaw, Poland. His father worked hard in a shop. Still, the family of eight lived in a cramped apartment. They barely had enough money for food. When Schmuel's father died, the family's money problems got worse. Schmuel pictured the years ahead; he knew he faced a weary life of hard work and little pay. The boy had a daring idea—he would run away to America! He had heard rumors that anything was possible there. He sold a few of his father's things and set out. He was sixteen years old.

How is Schmuel's story like other immigrant stories?

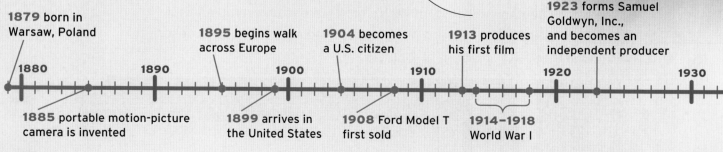

1879 born in Warsaw, Poland

1895 begins walk across Europe

1904 becomes a U.S. citizen

1913 produces his first film

1923 forms Samuel Goldwyn, Inc., and becomes an independent producer

1880 1890 1900 1910 1920 1930

1885 portable motion-picture camera is invented

1899 arrives in the United States

1908 Ford Model T first sold

1914–1918 World War I

Where would you go to live if you were in Sam's situation?

Alone and often hungry, Schmuel walked hundreds of miles to Germany. From there, he went to Birmingham, England, where his aunt lived. He took the name Sam Goldfish to sound more English. He thought he might stay in England. But Sam found that Birmingham was not all that different from Warsaw. His aunt and uncle struggled to make a living. Sam was not strong enough to do the hard jobs that he could get. As soon as he got enough money, he boarded a ship to Canada. From there, he trudged mile after mile through the snow. Finally, he crossed into Maine. He had made it to America!

Sam moved to Gloversville, a town in New York. Many Polish immigrants found jobs in the glove factories there. Sam did too at first. Then he saw something that gave him an idea.

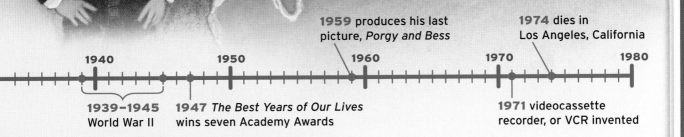

1959 produces his last picture, *Porgy and Bess*

1974 dies in Los Angeles, California

1940   1950   1960   1970   1980

1939–1945 World War II

1947 *The Best Years of Our Lives* wins seven Academy Awards

1971 videocassette recorder, or VCR invented

Scene Two . . .

The Kingsborough Hotel. A grand building made of brick and stone. Inside, a luxurious dining room where well-dressed, well-fed salesmen eat fancy meals. A weary young man in work clothes walks by the window.

Partner Jigsaw Technique Read a section of the biography with a partner and write down one connection you made. Be prepared to summarize your section and share the connection.

Sam wanted more than anything to live like the salesmen he saw at the Kingsborough Hotel. Like many European Jews, Sam had grown up speaking Yiddish. He began studying English at night. Then he offered his boss a deal—he would take the hardest sales route. He would sell to shops that had never bought his company's gloves. He would do it without pay, too, just to prove himself! Who could pass up that deal? Sam did prove himself. In a few years, he was one of the top glove salesmen. He didn't know it then, but his talent for making deals would help him make his place in history.

Was Sam's experience similar to other stories of immigrants you have heard of or read about?

By about 1913, Sam wanted to leave the glove business. But what was next? One day, with a little time on his hands, he stopped into a nickelodeon. A nickelodeon was a place that showed motion pictures.

Scene Three . . .

A few hundred seats stand in a room that feels like a large, dark cave. Suddenly, a WHIRRING sound as a film projector comes to life. A black-and-white image flickers on a white screen. A cowboy rides a galloping horse. A train barrels right toward the audience! The audience SCREAMS.

That was it! Sam knew right away that he wanted to be a part of this new art form. Early motion pictures were quite different from today's movies. They were in black and white, not color. They had no sound, and most of them were only ten or fifteen minutes long. They didn't really tell stories, but they did show lots of action. People were amazed just to see these moving pictures.

Have you read about other successful people like Sam? Who?

Sam wanted to make movies that told real stories, as stage plays did. These films would be longer, "feature-length" movies. In 1913, Sam and his partners made their first film in a small California town. Today, Hollywood is at the heart of the movie industry. But Sam's western was the first longer movie filmed there. It was a hit!

Sam changed his last name to Goldwyn. In a way, he and the movie business grew up together. Over time, movies added sound and color. Goldwyn found better stories to tell.

NICKELODE

NOW PLAYING

Goldwyn was hard to work with. He had strong ideas about how a movie should be made. Many other producers wanted mostly to make money, but Goldwyn wanted to make fine movies. That's just what he did. He found the best directors, he hired the most talented writers, and he used some of the biggest stars. He also created new stars. His masterpiece, *The Best Years of Our Lives*, won seven Academy Awards.

> Have you ever received an award that you worked hard for?

Scene Four . . .

1947. The Shrine Auditorium in Los Angeles. More than six thousand people clap wildly. On stage, a man in a formal suit blinks a few times. For a moment, he thinks back to his days in Warsaw. Then he smiles and holds his award high for all to see.

Goldwyn helped shape the movie business from its early days, just as he had worked hard to shape his own life. He died in 1974, a long, long way from his childhood home in Warsaw. But his movies are still played around the world.

Scene Five . . .

2010. Anywhere. A movie theater. A young girl watches an old movie by Samuel Goldwyn. Light from the movie flickers over her. Suddenly, she GASPS! An idea. . . .

How do you think this movie ends?

Think and Respond

Reflect and Write

- You and your partner have read sections of *Samuel Goldwyn, Picture This . . .* Discuss the connections each of you made.

- Choose a connection and write it on an index card. Share your ideas with a set of partners that read a different section from you.

Initial Consonants in Context

Look through *Samuel Goldwyn, Picture This . . .* to find all the words that begin with the consonants *g, m, p, f, r,* and *s.* Write down each word. Then use all of the words to write a paragraph about Samuel Goldwyn.

Turn and Talk

MAKE CONNECTIONS

Discuss in a small group what you have learned so far about making connections between something you are reading and what you know.

- What connections have you made as you read about Samuel Goldwyn?

- What do these connections help you understand about Samuel Goldwyn's life?

Work with a small group to discuss other connections.

Critical Thinking

With a partner discuss why Samuel Goldwyn came to the United States. Identify why Goldwyn left Poland and England. List ways that Goldwyn made a living at different times in his life.

Then write answers to these questions.

- Why do you think Goldwyn wanted to come to the United States?

- How did Goldwyn achieve success in the United States?

- How does this story support the idea that immigrants often come to the United States for economic reasons?

A Place For Us

Contents

Modeled Reading

Expository Coming to America: The Story of Immigration
by Betsy Maestro 36

Vocabulary
permanent, relocation, origin, regulate, necessities............... 38

Comprehension Strategy !
Determine Importance 40

Shared Reading

Historical Fiction Family Treasures
by Jerrill Parham 42

Word Study
Consonant Blends *sn-* and *-st* 44

Interactive Reading

Expository The World on Your Plate
by Neil Fairbairn 46

Vocabulary
belief, border, accompany, audience, nationality......52

Poem "Celebrating Our Roots: American Suitcase"
by Abby Jones 54

Word Study
Word Families... 56

Play The Fair by Sue Miller 58

COMING TO AMERICA
THE STORY OF IMMIGRATION

BY BETSY MAESTRO

ILLUSTRATED BY
SUSANNAH RYAN

INTERNATIONAL ARRIVALS

At Home in Little Havana

When my grandmother and I walk down the street in Miami's Little Havana, she closes her eyes. She says she can smell Cuba. All the **necessities** —the scents of rich coffee and the chicken and rice of her memory—are here.

She listens to guitar music through open windows. Snapping fingers **regulate** the beat. She enjoys the familiar language people speak as they pass by. She stops to listen to the tapping of dancing feet. She can hear Cuba.

When she opens her eyes, she sees the bright paintings on the sides of buildings. She likes the oranges and reds in the pictures for sale along the sidewalks. She smiles at the purple cabbages and yellow peppers in the markets. She says she can see her country of **origin** here.

At first, **relocation** was hard for her. Nothing felt **permanent**. She longed for Cuba. Now among the smells, sounds, and sights of Little Havana, she feels at home.

Structured Vocabulary Discussion

When your teacher says a vocabulary word, have the people in your group take turns saying the first word they think of. Continue until your teacher says, "Stop." Then have the last person who said a word explain how the word is related to the vocabulary word.

Throughout the week, add to your vocabulary journal entries. Record new insights and other words that relate to this week's vocabulary.

Picture It

Draw charts like these two in your vocabulary journal. Fill in the chart with things that are **permanent**.

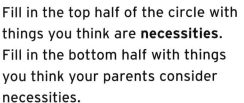

permanent

mountain

Fill in the top half of the circle with things you think are **necessities**. Fill in the bottom half with things you think your parents consider necessities.

My Ideas

sleep

necessities

My Parents' Ideas

39

Comprehension Strategy

Determine Importance

Not all information in a selection is of equal importance. To understand better what you read, learn to determine importance. First, look for important information at the beginning, middle, and end before getting to the overall information. Next separate the interesting information from the important information. Then, notice any text features, such as headings or graphs, that can help you decide what is important or unimportant information.

Think about the most IMPORTANT ideas.

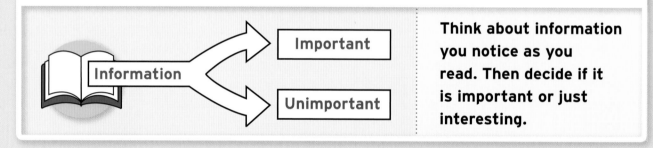

Think about information you notice as you read. Then decide if it is important or just interesting.

TURN AND TALK Listen as your teacher reads the following lines from *Coming to America.* The author writes about the many cultures in the United States. With a partner, discuss the important information.

• What is the main idea?

• What information is important to support the main idea?

• What information is interesting but not important to the main idea?

America has always been called a great "melting pot," where many cultures, or ways of life, have blended together. But today, Americans have also learned to celebrate their differences. There is a growing appreciation and understanding of the special character and unique contributions of each cultural or ethic group. Everyone, from the first Americans thousands of years ago to those who came only yesterday, has left a lasting mark on this great land.

TAKE IT WITH YOU Finding out what is important makes you a better reader. As you read other selections, try to separate important from unimportant information. Use a chart like this one to help you decide.

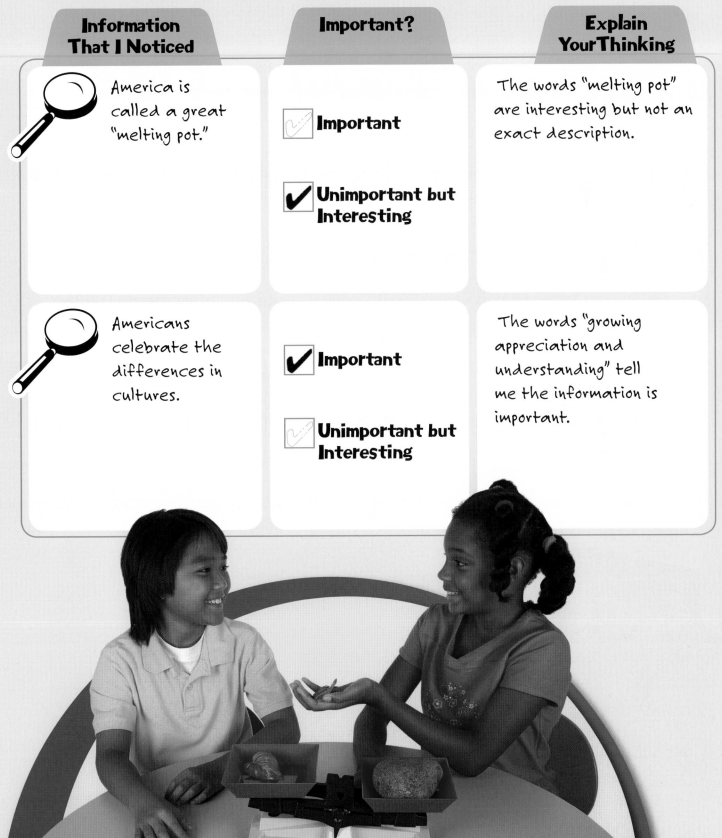

Information That I Noticed	Important?	Explain Your Thinking
America is called a great "melting pot."	☑ Important ✔ Unimportant but Interesting	The words "melting pot" are interesting but not an exact description.
Americans celebrate the differences in cultures.	✔ Important ☑ Unimportant but Interesting	The words "growing appreciation and understanding" tell me the information is important.

Family Treasures

by Jerrill Parham

Korea

Hana Koo liked her snug home in Korea. As she went inside, she touched the carving outside the door, as she often did. Her grandfather had made the detailed carving about 60 years earlier. Now, in 1906, Hana would be leaving it.

Hana walked over to a fine wooden chest. Its rich, deep wood was covered with snowy white bits of ox horn. The ox horn was part of a beautiful design of people, flowers, trees, and birds. Her grandfather had carved this chest, too.

Family stories told how Grandfather and Grandmother had built this house to hold their family. Now the family was moving to Hawaii. Hana's father had heard that Korean workers were being hired to work in the sugarcane fields of Hawaii. It was a chance to find a better life. But the family would have to leave Korea far behind. "Oh, family," whispered Hana, "I will miss this home and everything beautiful around it."

Mother saw Hana's sad face. She said warmly, "Don't worry, Hana. We will take our memories and ways of doing things to Hawaii. We'll take the chest with its family treasures, too.

"Now, Hana, I have a task for you. Father and I want us all to add things we've made to the chest. You know, important things that we and family after us will use."

Hana did know. Many of Grandfather and Grandmother's special things were stored in the chest. The family brought them out for important occasions. But what could Hana add? She thought for days. She watched Mother and Father place a beautiful pillow and bamboo cups in the chest.

One day, Hana rubbed her hand across the carving as she went outside. At last, she knew what to make!

Hana made a rubbing of the old carving. It showed a deer, a flower, and the vines that grew in Korea's mountains. The deer meant long life, and the flower meant friendliness. She added paint and the marks for each member of her family.

When the Koo family finally boarded the ship for Hawaii, Hana carried a secret promise to herself. Someday she would make a carving and proudly place it outside her new door. She hoped her family would touch it often.

Hawaii

Hao's Journal

September 15

The plane trip from Vietnam to California seemed like it would last forever! But we're here now. My father starts his new job with a high tech company next Monday. He is supposed to find fast ways for people to share information.

September 22

I am learning about my new home and remembering my old one. Today we got stuck in a traffic snarl on the way to the ocean. I could sniff the salt air for miles. The smell made me think of our beach house in Vietnam. Later, I managed to sneak a look at some distant mountains, and again I thought of home.

September 29

We had a special family night at school to share food from five countries. I was happy that my favorite noodle dish was a hit. I was even more pleased to taste my first tacos and mashed potatoes! I still miss Vietnam sometimes, but I like it here.

Consonant Blends
sn- and *-st*

Activity One

About Consonant Blends

A consonant blend is made up of two or more letters that are not vowels. These letters join to form one sound. Sometimes blends are at the beginning of a word, like the *sn-* in *snack*. Sometimes they are at the end of a word, like the *-st* in *lost*. As your teacher reads Hao's journal, listen carefully for words containing the blends *sn-* and *-st*.

Consonent Blends in Context

With a small group, reread the journal entries. In a chart like this, make a list of the words that have an *-st* or *sn-* consonant blend. Underline to show if the consonant blend appears at the beginning or end of the word.

CONSONANT BLEND	EXAMPLE
-st	la<u>st</u>

Activity Two

Explore Words Together

Work with a partner to add *sn-* or *-st* to the words at the right to make new words. Then list three more words you know that include *sn-* or *-st*. Discuss your list with another set of partners.

fore	out
ore	are
be	fir

Activity Three

Explore Words in Writing

Write a journal entry about an event in your own life. Use at least three *sn-* or *-st* words. Then share your journal entry with a partner. Have your partner circle the *sn-* and *-st* words.

The World on Your Plate

by Neil Fairbairn

The food we eat comes from all around the world. Foods arrived with the families who settled in North America over many hundreds of years. These foods have stories to tell. Let's listen to a few of them.

Stories from the Breakfast Table

Rise and shine. It's time for breakfast. Come join me at the table.

Orange Juice Nothing starts the day better than a glass of fresh juice. And nothing could be more American than orange juice. Right? Well, that's only partly true. In fact, long ago oranges grew only in China and India. Then traders brought them west to Europe. It was Christopher Columbus who carried the first orange seeds to America. That was over 500 years ago!

Oatmeal Are you hungry this morning? What about a bowl of hot oatmeal? Settlers from Scotland enjoyed oats cooked slowly in water to start the day. They planted oats on their first farms in the New World. Today we eat oatmeal just as those settlers did!

What clues help you determine the important information on this page?

Pancakes Still hungry? The first Dutch and British settlers brought their recipes for pancakes to the United States. At the time, Native Americans were already making their own pancakes out of corn. In fact, people all over the world cook pancakes.

How do the subheadings help you figure out important ideas on this page?

Yogurt Maybe you like a light breakfast. A fruit yogurt would be just right for you. Yogurt is a type of sour milk that people in Asia have eaten for centuries. Turkish people brought it with them to the United States. Yogurt is good for breakfast or as a snack, and it's good for you!

What's for Lunch?

Let's grab some lunch at a restaurant. Here's one with a special kid's menu. The choices all come from different parts of the world.

Pizza What about pizza? Long ago, Italian bakers made flat bread in very hot ovens. Then they discovered a new vegetable from America. It was called the tomato. One day someone made a sauce out of tomatoes and baked it on the bread. The result was delicious! Top it with cheese and you have the pizza we know today. Italians who came to North America brought the pizza with them.

Menu

Slice of cheese pizza with salad

Frankfurter with mustard and relish

Tortilla wrap with beans and chicken

Toasted bagel with cream cheese

Two-Word Technique
Write down two words that reflect your thoughts about each page. Discuss them with your partner.

Frankfurters Maybe you'd prefer the frankfurter. You may know it as a hot dog or a wiener. Whatever the name, it's that sausage in a long roll. Germans who came to America in the 1800s loved their sausages. They named this one after their city of Frankfurt. Other Americans found that the frankfurter tasted great. What's a baseball game without a hot dog?

Tortillas The pizza and the frankfurter came across the ocean. The tortilla crossed the border from Mexico. It's another type of pancake—but it's different from the ones you have for breakfast. Tortillas are made from corn or wheat flour. They are very thin. They're great for wraps.

Bagels When Jewish people came from Europe to live in the United States, the bagel came with them. It's a circle of bread with a hole in the middle. Bagels are chewy and filling. You may like them best plain. You can also get bagels with seeds, onions, or raisins. Bagels are tasty cut in half and spread with butter or cream cheese. They also make great sandwiches or toast.

What information on this page is interesting but not important?

Dinner Time!

Does all this traveling make you hungry? I surely hope so—it's time for dinner.

Pasta What about a heaping plate of steaming pasta for dinner? Italians who traveled to the United States brought their love of pasta with them. Pasta is a very simple food to make. All you have to do is add eggs or water to flour to form a paste. (*Pasta* means "paste" in Italian.) Then you roll it out and cut it into shapes. What shapes would you choose? The strand form of spaghetti is one of the most popular shapes, but there are many others—ribbons, spirals, wheels, and tubes, to name a few. Thick or thin, straight or curly, no matter what the shape, pasta tastes great.

> What important information did you notice on this page? Explain.

Rice Did you notice how important grains are in our diet? Many of our foods, like pasta, pancakes, or bagels, are made from wheat. Another very important grain is rice. In much of the world, people eat rice every day. Chinese immigrants helped make rice dishes popular in the United States. One of the best-known Chinese dishes is fried rice. Rice goes well with lots of food, from meats to vegetables. How do you like to eat your rice?

Couscous (koos-koos) What about something different for dinner? Have you ever tried couscous? Couscous comes from North Africa and is the national dish of Morocco. It is popular in many countries. Couscous looks like tiny brown grains, but it is made from flour. It is actually small balls of pasta. When cooked, it looks a little like rice. You eat it with meat or vegetable stew. Couscous is both filling and delicious.

What is the most important idea you have read in this selection?

Crepes (krayps) Did you leave room for dessert? Crepes are a very thin type of pancake from France. You can eat crepes dusted with sugar and filled with fruit. (Did you notice how many pancakes there are? You could eat a different type for every meal!)

People have come from many nations to live in the United States. Their food has traveled with them. Next time you sit down to eat, have a close look at your plate. Can you see a nationality in your food? Can you see many nationalities?

Think and Respond

Reflect and Write

- You and your partner have read *The World on Your Plate*. You wrote two words on sticky notes. Read the words you wrote to your partner.

- Discuss why you chose those words and whether those words relate to an important or unimportant detail in the article.

Consonant Blends in Context

Reread *The World on Your Plate* to find examples of words that begin with the consonant blend *sn-* or end with *-st*. Write down the words you find, and then share them with a partner. Work together to think of other words.

Turn and Talk

DETERMINE IMPORTANCE

Discuss with a partner what you have learned so far about how to determine importance.

- How do you determine importance?

- How does determining importance make you a better reader?

Find one important and one unimportant detail in *The World on Your Plate*. Explain to a partner why each detail is important or unimportant.

Critical Thinking

Discuss in a small group the cultural origins of the foods mentioned in *The World on Your Plate*. Write a list of the foods discussed and the origin of each one. Then discuss each of these questions.

- Which foods are found in different forms in several cultures?

- How does this selection support the idea that the United States is home to people from many different cultures? Explain your answer.

Dance to the Music

To: Susan From: Beth

Hi Susan,

The L.A. Salsa Kids put on quite a show last night. I expected it would be like any other school program. I quickly realized *that* **belief** was wrong!

The dancers not only kick up their heels, they click them to a Latin beat. The costumes are bright, and great musicians **accompany** the dancing kids.

I tried to guess the **nationality** of each dance. The dances came from many Latin America countries. My favorite dance was the salsa from Cuba.

You might think the group comes from south of the **border,** but it started in Los Angeles. The group's aim is to interest both dancers and the **audience** in Latin dance. They sure caught my interest! The music made me want to get up and dance.

The L.A. Salsa Kids hold a search for dancers as young as eleven years old. Let's check out their Web site. See you at school.

Beth

Structured Vocabulary Discussion

Work with a partner to fill in the following blanks. When you have finished, share your answers with the class. Be sure you can explain how the words are related.

Look is to *notice* as *crowd* is to _____.

Bug is to *insect* as *opinion* is to _____.

Club is to *membership* as *country* is to _____.

Throughout the week, add to your vocabulary journal entries. Record new insights and other words that relate to this week's vocabulary.

Picture It

Draw a chart like this in your vocabulary journal. Fill in the spaces with pairs of things that can **accompany** each other.

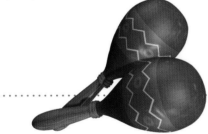

accompany	bacon and eggs

Draw a graphic organizer like this in your vocabulary journal. Fill in the arms of the star with things that might have an **audience**.

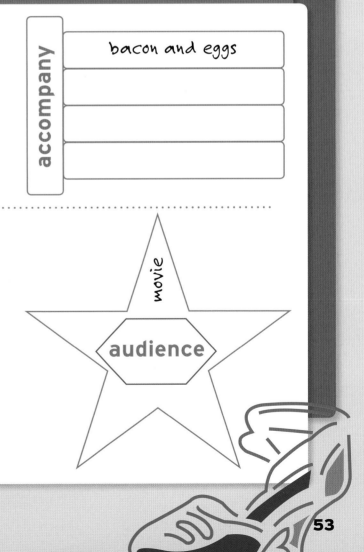

movie

audience

53

Celebrating Our Roots

American Suitcase

by Abby Jones

In my suitcase

    a culture is packed

      a tradition folded

        a story wrapped

I am from China, Mexico, Haiti, France . . .

In my suitcase

    I bring understandings

      I transport ideas

        I carry a history

I am African, Indian, English, Czech . . .

In my suitcase,

From Ukraine, from Korea, from Spain,

Dreams I wear every day accompany

    my fears

        my language

            my art

                my religion

                    my food

my love for this culture of many.

I am American.

Fourth Grade News

World Dance Exhibition

by Mario Donatello

Last week, our class put on a world dance exhibition for our school's parent organization. Our teacher, Miss Watkins, helped us pick a set of dances from different parts of the world. We had been practicing for the past month, and we were really glad to show off what we had learned.

The show started with a dance from Greece. This one was really fun. The music was fast. The dancers formed a circle and the steps included a lot of quick turning.

The next dance was from Bolivia. The dancers dressed in ponchos and wore masks in the shape of animals. There was a monkey, a pig, a cat, and a parrot. Bolivian music features flutes and drums. It has a unique sound.

The last dance was a dragon dance that came from China. The performers used poles to hold up a big dragon puppet. The dragon wiggled, twisted, and spun in time with the music. The audience seemed very impressed!

Word Families

Activity One

About Word Families

A word family is a group of rhyming words that all end with the same sounds and letters. Sometimes you can add one letter to the rhyming word ending to make a new word. For example, you can add *b* before *ig* to make *big*. You can also add a consonant blend. For example, you can add *sn* before *ag* to make *snag*. As your teacher reads *World Dance Exhibition*, listen for the word families.

Word Families in Context

With a small group, reread *World Dance Exhibition*. Then fill in the chart with another pair of rhyming words from the article and a list of other words from the same word family.

RHYMING WORDS FROM ARTICLE	MORE RHYMING WORDS
fun, spun	pun, run

Activity Two

that	spot
when	chop
twig	shrug

Explore Words Together

Look at the words on the right with a partner. Work together to make new words by replacing the consonant blend of each word with other consonants. List the words.

Activity Three

Explore Words in Writing

Using words form the activity above, write two lines of rhyming poetry. Share your poetry with a partner.

THE Fair

by Sue Miller

Characters:

Danny	Tyree	Sanjay	Gina	Vance
Megan	Myra	Nikki	Annie	Emilio

All students are fourth grade members of the school's International Club. The principal has asked the club to plan a culture fair for the school. They have stayed after school for a planning meeting.

How does this play remind you of school plays you have been in? Describe your role.

Setting: *A classroom*   **Time:** *Present day*

VANCE, GINA, MYRA, EMILIO, ANNIE, SANJAY, and NIKKI are sitting around a table. TYREE is standing at the chalkboard. MEGAN and DANNY are coming through the door and carrying a stack of books each.

TYREE (*shaking his head*): Wow! Did you take every book in the library?

MEGAN (*frowning*): We can't plan if we don't know what we are talking about!

EMILIO: How hard can it be? It's not like it's a science project! We just need ideas.

MEGAN: If we're going to plan a culture fair, we need to know *everything*! Ms. James said that we need to cover all the bases. Dances, music, dress, beliefs, food—everything!

DANNY (*licking his lips and rubbing his stomach*): I could really get into this project if I had food. A spring roll . . . noodles . . . something. Anything! I'm starving.

NIKKI (*rolling her eyes*): You're always starving! But you have a point. Your grandparents are from Vietnam. When you think of a snack, you think of spring rolls. My Italian Nana would say, "Have some pizza."

DANNY: Hey, I like pizza. I love pizza. I WANT SOME PIZZA! (*Danny fakes going crazy.*)

The others laugh.

What do you know about food from another culture?

TYREE (*still standing at the chalkboard*): Okay. So, we want a food table at the fair. (*He writes* Food *on the board.*) How many different kinds of food should we have?

GINA: Well, Italian and Vietnamese. We should also have Mexican.

EMILIO: My mom's a great cook. Maybe she can help me make apple empanadas. They're kind of like little apple pies. She makes her own dough.

GINA: Now, I'm hungry! My mom is from Jamaica, and my dad is from Haiti. In Jamaica, my mom made jerked goat. Here, she uses chicken.

VANCE: So, why was the goat a jerk? Did he eat all her flowers, or something?

GINA: *J–E–R–K–E–D*, not *jerk*, silly. It's just really spicy and hot. We should also do Indian food. Sanj's family is from India. Sanj, what do you like to eat?

SANJAY: Me? I like pizza. But it can't have meat on it. My family doesn't eat meat. A lot of Indian families don't.

MYRA: What about Filipino food? I think we should get a bunch of recipes, and make a display. My mom makes a great grilled squid.

MEGAN (*looking surprised*): Wow! Squid! Let's talk about dancing. I want to include Irish folk dancing. Annie and I are taking a step dancing class.

ANNIE nods her head in agreement.

TYREE (*looking puzzled*): You have to take classes to step? That's weird!

Say Something Technique
Take turns reading a section of text, covering it up, and then saying something about it to your partner. You may say any thought or idea that the text brings to your mind.

What traditional folk dances from other countries have you seen?

ANNIE: No, Ty. Step is a kind of Irish dance. It's really fun, and the costumes are really, really neat. Megan and I could bring our costumes for the fair. Maybe we could even do a little dance. It would be fun to perform for an audience.

VANCE: Cool! I'm part Navajo. I've danced in a couple of powwows. They're like fairs for different Indian tribes. I've got a cool outfit. I wouldn't mind showing people a dance. I won a competition last summer. My dad was really proud of me.

TYREE: All right! That sounds cool. Does your costume have feathers and everything?

VANCE: It sure does—lots of feathers. It also has beads. My mom made it. It's great!

NIKKI: What about music? Isn't your uncle in a mariachi band, Emilio?

EMILIO: He sure is.

Have you heard music from another culture? Explain.

NIKKI: Maybe you could interview him. You could ask him questions about how mariachi bands got started, and maybe he could play little bits of songs. We could set up a recording that people could play to get information about music from Mexico.

SANJAY: That's a cool idea, Nik. My dad can play the sitar. It's kind of like an Indian guitar. He was in a band before he married my mom. His sitar has 17 strings! Maybe I could interview him.

TYREE: *(looking really excited)* Yeah! And I could interview my dad. He's in a zydeco band. He plays the accordion. Zydeco is kind of like Cajun music. It was started by the Creoles in Louisiana. My dad is Creole. That means he's French and African American.

DANNY: Awesome! I don't know any musicians, but I do take martial arts. I'm learning Cuong Nhu. It's the Vietnamese form of karate. *Cuong Nhu* is Vietnamese for *hard* and *soft*. Many Asians believe that the world is made up of opposites—yin and yang. Cuong Nhu uses hard and soft techniques—opposites!

> How are the foods, music, and sports in this play similar to your experiences?

ANNIE: How do you know all that?

DANNY: My instructor teaches us. You can't do martial arts without learning all this stuff.

VANCE: I know what you mean. Emilio and I take Tae Kwon Do. Our instructor teaches us things like that. He's always saying we need to search for the right path in life! Speaking of martial arts, we've got to get moving. Mom will be here to pick Emilio and me up for Tae Kwon Do.

DANNY: Yeah, I've got to go, too.

VANCE, DANNY, and EMILIO stand up and head for the door.

TYREE: Guys, we need to have information on different beliefs from other cultures. Yin and yang is only one belief.

DANNY and EMILIO continue out the door. VANCE stops and turns.

VANCE *(groaning)*: Later, dude. I'm *not* missing my class! By the way, Tae Kwon Do comes from Korea!

Think and Respond

Reflect and Write

- You and your partner have read *The Fair*. Discuss the thoughts and ideas the play made you think about.

- Choose three ideas that demonstrate connections to text, to self, and to the world. Write these three ideas on index cards. On the back of the cards, explain the connections. Then share your cards with your partner.

Word Families in Context

Reread *The Fair* to find examples of words from word families that end in *ap, at, et, en, ig, op, ot, ug,* and *un*. Write down the words you find. Then share them with a partner. Work together to write a short poem about cultures using several of the word families.

Turn and Talk

MAKE CONNECTIONS

Discuss with a partner what you have learned so far about making connections.

- What does it mean to make connections when you read?

- How does making connections help you as you read?

- Think about *The Fair*. What connections can you make between the play and things you already know?

Choose one connection you made while reading. Explain that connection to a partner.

Critical Thinking

Talk about the different cultures mentioned by the characters in *The Fair*. Think about what each group has contributed to American culture. List the cultures discussed. List the different contributions, such as food, music, and dances, of each group mentioned. Then answer each of these questions.

- How does this selection support the idea that the United States is home to people from many different cultures?

- How have different immigrant groups enriched American culture? Explain your answers.

あいきみ つらへ
ふくきそき うき
こを む
小箕芳枝

あられもまよ
をくらの
こを むー

こをすまよまれ
きひきの
床

from *A Picture Book of Selected Insects*, 1788
Kitagawa Utamaro (c.1753–1806)

人つてにくもんと首と
あ
り
け
る
か
り
ま
れ
つ
ら
へ

娃
宿
室
販
筆

THEME **3** **So Many Kinds of Animals**

THEME **4** **Seeds, Fruits, and Flowers**

Viewing

The artist who created this woodblock print lived more than 300 years ago in Japan. Creating a woodblock print took the artist many hours to carve the wood and then to print one color at a time. During Utamaro's lifetime, he created more than 2000 prints. His work was very popular.

1. What plants and animals can you see in the print?

2. What do you think might happen next to the insect?

3. Why do you think the artist included the big leaf?

In This UNIT

In this unit, you will read about the characteristics of animals and plants. You will learn how these characteristics help living things survive.

Contents

So Many Kinds of Animals

Modeled Reading

Mystery Seal by Judy Allen 68

Vocabulary
variety, species, researchers, abandon, definite 70

Comprehension Strategy
Infer 72

Shared Reading

Expository Weird Animals by Ann Weil 74

Word Study
Long Vowels 76

Interactive Reading

Humor Slimy, Spiny Riddles by Alice Leonhardt 78

Vocabulary
characteristic, identify, categorize,
invertebrate, vertebrate 84

Poem "Vertebrate or Invertebrate—What's my ID?"
by Ruth Siburt 86

Grammar
Nouns 88

Encyclopedia Animals by Renée Carver 90

SEAL

by Judy Allen *Illustrated by* Tudor Humphries

Critical Listening

Critical listening is listening to compare and contrast ideas in the story. Listen to the focus questions your teacher will read to you.

The Vanishing Mediterranean Monk SEAL

Q **What is a Mediterranean monk seal?**

A The Mediterranean monk seal is a **species** of seal that lives along the coasts of Europe and North Africa.

Q **How many Mediterranean monk seals are there?**

A **Researchers** do not know the **definite** number. There may be fewer than 500 left. Fifty years ago, there were about five thousand!

Q **What threats do the seals face?**

A Humans catch the same fish that monk seals eat. Also, fishermen sometimes kill seals. In addition, the water the seals live in has become dirty.

Q **Why do the seals leave their homes?**

A Monk seals **abandon** their homes when people get too close. Divers, boaters, tourists, and home construction along beaches all cause seals to leave their homes.

Q **What can people do to save the seals?**

A People can do a **variety** of things to help the seals. Many governments, for instance, have passed laws to protect the seals and the wild areas where they live.

Structured Vocabulary Discussion

When your teacher says a vocabulary word, write all of the words the vocabulary word makes you think of. When your teacher says, "Stop," share your words with a partner. Take turns explaining to each other why the words on your list popped into your mind.

Throughout the week, add to your vocabulary journal entries. Record new insights and other words that relate to this week's vocabulary.

Picture It

Copy this word web in your vocabulary journal. Fill in the empty circles with things that **researchers** study.

seals

researchers

Copy this chart into your vocabulary journal. Fill in the left side with things that are **definite**. Fill in the right side with things that are not **definite**.

definite	
yes	**no**
my age	weather

Comprehension Strategy!

Infer

To infer is to figure things out based on what you read and what you already know. Making inferences, or inferring, helps you understand what the author may not directly state.

> **When you INFER, you use your own ideas to better understand what you read.**
>
>
>
> **Combine what you read and what you already know.**

TURN AND TALK In *Seal*, Stefanos asks Jenny not to reveal the location of the seals. Listen as your teacher reads the following lines from *Seal*. With a partner, discuss what you can *infer* by answering the following questions.

- What does Stefanos know about the seals?
- What do you know about wild animals that need protection from humans?
- How would you feel in this situation?

Stefanos kept the boat steady and spoke to her softly. "I know what you found," he said. "Their last hiding place. I must tell you that if they are disturbed the mothers may abandon the babies, or even kill them!"

"I didn't disturb them," said Jenny, horrified.

"No," said Stefanos, "but will you betray them?"

"My family wouldn't hurt them!" said Jenny.

"Wouldn't they want to look?" said Stefanos. "Wouldn't they dive down, just once? And wouldn't others hear of it, and come out to see?"

TAKE IT WITH YOU Making inferences will help you understand what you read. As you read other selections, combine the information that you read with things you already know to form inferences. Use a chart like the one below to make inferences.

In the Text

Stefanos speaks softly to Jenny about the seals and their hiding place.

In My Head

Stefanos doesn't want anyone to hear him talk to Jenny. He doesn't want anyone to find out about the seals and their hiding place.

In the Text

Stefanos knows the seals' hiding place, and he knows what will happen if people disturb them. He knows there are not many seals left.

In My Head

The seals need special protection. Stefanos wants to protect the seals.

Weird ANIMALS

by Ann Weil

Many animals puzzle us because they look and behave in very strange ways. Take a look at these four weird animals—three dogs and a mouse. They are unlike any animals you have ever seen!

Bush Dog

Bush dogs are rare wild dogs that live in Central and South America. These strange dogs sound like birds and swim like fish. Their "bark" sounds like a whistle or chirp. Unlike most dogs, bush dogs dive under the surface of the water, where their webbed feet help them swim.

Raccoon Dog

The raccoon dog has a face like a raccoon and sleeps in the winter like a bear! This strange dog is not like *any* family pet. It does not even bark. The dogs come from Asia, where people prize them for their thick fur. In the 1920s, Russian farmers began raising raccoon dogs for their fur. Some animals escaped into the wild. As a result, raccoon dogs have spread across Europe.

Maned Wolf

The maned wolf lives in South America. It gets its name from the dark, thick fur that runs down its back. It is also known as the stilt-legged fox because of its long, thin legs. But this animal is neither a wolf nor a fox. The maned wolf is really a dog, in the same family of animals as the bush and raccoon dogs.

Grasshopper Mouse

The grasshopper mouse lives in North America. Unlike an ordinary mouse, it is a mighty hunter with sharp teeth and big jaw muscles! Grasshopper mice like to eat grasshoppers, insects, lizards, and scorpions. It does not squeak. It stands up on its back legs and HOWLS! Its roar can be heard more than 100 yards away!

**Weird Dogs:
Weight Comparisons**

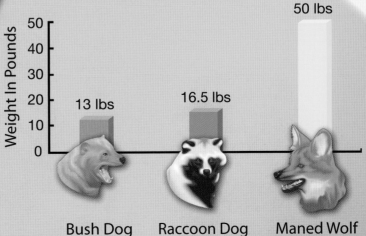

Weight In Pounds

50 lbs

16.5 lbs

13 lbs

Bush Dog   Raccoon Dog   Maned Wolf

A Coral Reef Adventure

August 15, 9:30 A.M.

For my ninth birthday, my parents gave me two hours of snorkeling lessons. Today I explore my first coral reef. Every time I have a break, I will record what I have seen in my journal.

August 15, 10:30 A.M.

At first, the coral reef looked like it's decorated with plants. As I got closer, I realized that many of the shapes were really animals.

August 15, 11:00 A.M.

I swam past some tiny jellyfish. They don't have even one bone.

August 15, 11:30 A.M.

The reef is a moving rainbow of color! I saw one fish with a bright blue fin down its spine. My dad said it was a parrotfish.

August 15, 12:00 P.M.

I got a picture of a seahorse! It looks like a bumpy, moving letter s with a face. I even saw an eel. It looks like a long tube. It was amazing to get close to creatures I've seen only in science books.

Long Vowels

Activity One

About Long Vowels

A vowel usually has the long sound when a consonant and silent e come after it, such as *bike*. As your teacher reads *A Coral Reef Adventure*, listen for the long-vowel sounds.

Long Vowels in Context

With a partner, reread the journal to find words with long-vowel sounds followed by a consonant and a silent e. Write each word you find in a chart like the one below. Underline the vowel-consonant-silent e combination and say the word out loud. Then think of another word with the same sound.

WORD	RHYMING WORD
sh<u>ape</u>	tape

Activity Two

Explore Words Together

The list on the right contains words with a long vowel followed by a consonant and a silent e. Change each word to another long-vowel word replacing the consonants with other consonants. For example, change the word *take* into *late* or *plate*. Talk with a partner about your list of old and new words.

take	lone
theme	cube
like	globe

Activity Three

Explore Words in Writing

Choose three of the words with the long-vowel combination that you listed.
Write a sentence using each of the words you chose.
Share your favorite sentence with a partner.

Slimy, Spiny RIDDLES

by Alice Leonhardt

SLIME LAB

"Welcome, welcome, Pete and Kate," Uncle Isaac said. "Welcome to the Sea Star, Leech, Insect, Millipede, and Earthworm Laboratory, otherwise known as SLIME."

"SLIME?" Kate repeated. "All those animals aren't slimy."

"True, but they are all special animals that we study." Professor Isaac Lane, also known as Uncle Isaac, led the two kids into his lab.

Kate and Pete glanced around. Uncle Isaac's lab was filled with aquariums and terrariums. They were stacked on shelves and crowded on tables.

"Come, come." Quickly, Uncle Isaac started down an aisle. "I have much to show you. Your mother said you were doing a report for a class project?"

"Yes. We have to identify the animals we're studying." Kate stopped and peered into a lighted aquarium. "But there are so many different kinds that Pete and I get confused."

What is one way to identify different animals?

78

"I hope I can help," Uncle Isaac said. "Here at SLIME we study slimy, spiny animals—many of them insects—because insects make up two thirds of all animal species." Uncle Isaac bent over a terrarium and tapped on the screen covering the top. "Insects include these little guys."

"What do you mean 'these little guys'?" Pete asked, peering into the terrarium. "I don't see anything but sticks and bark."

"Perhaps a riddle will help. *We're brown and green and although we can grow as long as 13 inches, you may never see us.*"

"The trail of dirty socks in Pete's bedroom?" Kate guessed, laughing.

Suddenly, Pete noticed a brown insect clinging to a branch. "A walking stick! I couldn't see it because it's camouflaged."

"Right you are, Pete," Uncle Isaac said. "Walking sticks are one of the longest insects. When they hatch from their eggs, they hide in leaves, so they're usually green. Only later do they turn brown. Now try and guess this next animal. *I eat almost anything including glue and hair.*"

"That's easy," Kate said. "Our dog, Skippy."

"Not quite. Perhaps a second clue will help. *I can be frozen, then thawed, and still be alive.*"

Why do you think it is important for insects to be able to hide?

Say Something Technique Take turns reading a section of text, covering it up, and then saying something about it to your partner. You may say any thought or idea that the text brings to your mind.

Pete guessed, "A monster in a movie?"

"A cockroach!" Uncle Isaac pointed to a terrarium full of shiny, reddish-brown insects. "Cockroaches live almost anywhere. They can slow down their heart rate. That's one reason they can survive when frozen."

"Here's another riddle: *I have 4,000 muscles but can't lift a finger.*"

"A weightlifter?" Pete guessed.

"Nope." Uncle Isaacs's eyes twinkled when he stopped in front of a terrarium. A caterpillar was busily munching a leaf. "It's a caterpillar. A caterpillar needs all those muscles to move its six legs and its 6 to 8 prolegs, which are leg-like walking stubs.

Now let's move on to my favorite animal." Uncle Isaac hurried down the aisle to an aquarium. *"What's slimy and helps heal a bruised, puffy eye?"*

Kate raised her hand. "A hunk of frozen steak."

"A leech!" Uncle Isaac plucked out a fat, slick, wormlike creature. "Isn't it a beauty?"

"Yuck!" Pete jumped back. "I thought leeches sucked blood."

"They do. Humans have used leeches in medicine for centuries. Today doctors mainly use them after some tricky operations. The leech sucks the extra blood from the wound to reduce swelling." Uncle Isaac put the leech back into the aquarium.

How do leeches help doctors?

80

"Here's another riddle," he said as he walked over to a dirt-filled bin. *What turns garbage into black gold?*"

"Nothing does, Uncle Isaac," Kate said, giggling.

"Well, maybe not black *gold*—except to a gardener."

Pete was bent over, looking into the bin. "All I see are earthworms."

"Hundreds of them, eating my leftovers from lunch. They munch their way through banana skins and lettuce leaves. Then they leave rich, black castings for our garden."

Why are earthworms important?

"Any more riddles, Uncle Isaac?" Kate asked.

"Yes. *What do you call a beautiful celebrity from the ocean?*"

Pete and Kate shrugged.

"A sea *star*!" Uncle Isaac pointed to an aquarium filled with bubbling water and rocks. "Also known as a starfish."

Kate bent closer. "I see them, clinging to the rocks. So many different sizes and colors: red, yellow, purple. But all shaped like stars."

"Those are their 'arms,' called rays," Uncle Isaac explained. "Most sea stars have five rays. But some, like the sun star, have as many as fifty rays."

"Uh, oh. We need to get home and start working on our project," Kate said.

Pete closed his notebook. "I sure wrote down a lot of good information about animals."

"A *special* group of animal," Uncle Isaac said. "All the animals we study at SLIME have one main characteristic in common."

"Huh?" Pete scratched his head. "All the animals are so different."

Kate nodded in agreement.

Uncle Isaac grinned. "Perhaps one last riddle will help: *We make up more than 95 percent of all animal species. Yet we don't have the backbone to stand up for ourselves and tell the world we're the greatest.*"

"No backbone!" Pete and Kate shouted together.

"That's correct," Uncle Isaac exclaimed. "All the animals at SLIME are invertebrates—the most wonderful animals on Earth!"

What is the main way that invertebrates differ from vertebrates?

Think and Respond

Reflect and Write

- You and your partner have read sections of *Slimy, Spiny Riddles*. Discuss the responses you had.

- Choose one response that helped you infer something. Write the response and the inference it led to on an index card. On the back of the card, write how the response helped you make the inference.

Long Vowels in Context

Reread *Slimy, Spiny Riddles* to find examples of long vowels. Write down the words you find. Have a contest with a partner to see who can find the most words with long vowel sounds. Then select three of the words to use in sentences. Share your favorite sentence with your partner.

Turn and Talk

INFER

Discuss with a partner what have you learned so far about making inferences, or inferring.

- What does it mean to infer something? How do you make an inference?

- How does making inferences help you understand what you read?

Choose one inference you made while reading *Slimy, Spiny Riddles*. Explain that inference to a partner.

Critical Thinking

Think about the animals described in *Slimy, Spiny Riddles*. Discuss with a partner the ways that the animals are similar and different. Choose one creature from the story and write its name on a piece of paper. Write its characteristics beside its name. Then discuss these questions.

- Why is it important to classify animals by their characteristics?

- What one characteristic links all of the animals in the laboratory?

- How does this story show the importance of classification of animals?

What's New?

Did you know that scientists are still discovering new animals? They are! One of the first things they do when they discover a new animal is to **categorize** it. Does it have a backbone, or doesn't it?

Many new finds do not have a backbone. Such an animal is an **invertebrate**. This is not surprising. Only about 5 percent of all known animals have backbones!

Sometimes new species show up in the strangest places. Scientists were able to **identify** a new centipede right in New York City!

Scientists still occasionally find a **vertebrate**, too. They discovered a new monkey in India. They were quite surprised. The country has a very large population and shrinking wild areas.

Surprising discoveries are what keep the hunt exciting. Scientists never know when they will find an animal with a new **characteristic**.

Arunachal Macaque discovered in India

Structured Vocabulary Discussion

Work with a partner to complete the following sentences about your vocabulary words.

Categorize and **identify** are similar because they both . . .

Vertebrate and **invertebrate** are different because . . .

Throughout the week, add to your vocabulary journal entries. Record new insights and other words that relate to this week's vocabulary.

Picture It

Copy the word circle into your vocabulary journal. Put a **characteristic** of humans in each outer space.

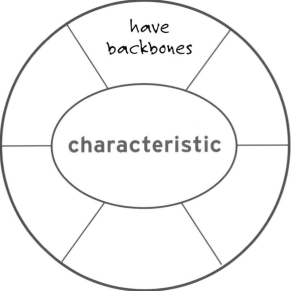

have backbones

characteristic

Copy this table into your vocabulary journal. Think of six animals. **Categorize** the animals as either **vertebrate** or **invertebrate**.

Vertebrate	Invertebrate
dog	beetle

Vertebrate or Invertebrate— What's My ID?

by Ruth Siburt

Can you *ID* me?

I hatch from a cocoon but do not fly.

I love still waters and hate the dry.

I have sharp teeth in my grin.

I use those teeth to bite through skin.

Scientists categorize me as a parasite.

You won't even feel it when I bite.

My body's divided into thirty-four parts.

Drs. still use me to heal what hurts.

Can you *ID* me?

Can you *ID* me?

I live in burrows cool and deep.

I roam at night, by day I sleep.

I carry my food in clever pockets.

When I leap, I'm like a furry rocket.

I eat small seeds and I never drink water.

I'm named for a creature from Aus., the "land down-under."

My bones are delicate and fine.

My eyes, by night, really shine.

Can you *ID* me?

A Day at The Zoo

Dear Mom and Dad,

Today Grandma and Grandpa took me to the National Zoo. I saw not only my first giant pandas, but also my first baby panda. Most baby pandas are born in the wilderness of China. This baby is the first to be born at the zoo and live for more than a few days!

The female weighs 250 pounds. Her baby weighed a quarter pound at birth. I've eaten hamburgers bigger than that!

When the baby was tiny, the mother stayed inside with it. Grandma says that the male didn't pay much attention to the baby until it could walk and climb.

Now the baby is six months old and can leave the family's structure. I watched it climb all over trees and rocks in the panda yard.

The baby's playtime gives the mother time for a long lunch. She can snack on bamboo, just as she did in the wilderness.

I had a wonderful day. I hope you'll have time to see the pandas when you come to pick me up.

Love,

Mark

Grammar *Nouns*

Activity One

About Nouns

A noun names a person, place, or thing. Most nouns, such as *boy*, *zoo*, *tree*, and *hope*, refer to general persons, places, things, or ideas. A proper noun refers to specific persons, places, and things, such as the *National Zoo* or *Mark*. As your teacher reads Mark's letter, listen for the nouns.

Nouns in Context

With a partner, read *A Day at the Zoo*. Find as many nouns as you can and write them in the correct category in a chart like the one below.

PEOPLE OR ANIMALS	PLACES	THINGS
panda	zoo	structure

Activity Two

Explore Words Together

laughter   alligator
doctor   station
fact   Maine

The list on the right contains nouns. With your partner, determine whether each noun is a person (or animal), place, or thing. Then together think of two additional nouns for each category.

Activity Three

Explore Words in Writing

Brainstorm a list of nouns that could fit in a letter about pandas. Then using your list, write two more sentences to add to Mark's letter about his visit to the zoo.

ANIMALS

by Renée Carver

Animal Kingdom

Scientists divide the living world into groups. Each group shares certain traits. Such groupings make it easier to study and compare living things. The largest kind of group is called a kingdom. All animals are considered part of the animal kingdom.

The Variety of Animal Life The list of the world's animals is very long. Mammals, birds, and fish are in this group. So are lizards, snakes, and frogs. Insects and worms are also animals. So are sponges, crabs, and jellyfish. In fact, scientists have named over one million animals. Scientists believe there are millions more still to be discovered.

Classifying Animals Animals are classified as either invertebrates or vertebrates. An invertebrate is an animal without a backbone. Insects are in this group. So are worms, sponges, crabs, and jellyfish. A vertebrate is an animal with a backbone. Mammals are in this group. So are birds, fish, lizards, snakes, and frogs. Animals with backbones make up only 5 percent of the animal kingdom.

What information on this page is important? How do you know?

Invertebrates

Most animals are invertebrates. Members of this group live almost everywhere on Earth. Many call the ocean home. Others survive in hot, sandy deserts. Invertebrates come in a wide range of sizes and shapes. A butterfly is an invertebrate. So is an ant or a crab. Many are so small you need a microscope to see them. Others, like the giant squid, are huge. Yet all share one characteristic. They have no backbone. Scientists divide invertebrates into two groups—those with soft bodies and those with hard bodies.

Soft-Bodied Invertebrates   Worms and jellyfish

are examples of soft-bodied invertebrates. Worms are long, thin creatures without any arms or legs. Some worms are round like a piece of string. Others are flat like a ribbon. Some worms have segmented bodies. Many worms have fluid inside their bodies. The fluid works like air in a tire to help the worm keep its shape.

What clues help you determine important information on this page?

Animal Characteristics

- Most animals have many cells.

- Most animals can move freely from place to place at some point in their lives.

- Animals have sense organs that make them aware of what is around them.

- Animals cannot make their own food. They get energy by eating other organisms.

- Most animals need a mate to reproduce.

Read, Cover, Remember, Retell Technique With a partner, take turns reading as much text as you can cover with your hand. Then cover up what you read and retell the information to your partner.

Jellyfish belong to a different group of soft-bodied invertebrates. Animals in this group all have tentacles around their mouths that can sometimes reach out and sting things.

Hard-Bodied Invertebrates A sponge looks like a floppy bag stuck in one place. You might think it is soft-bodied. However, tiny pieces of hard material hold up the bodies of most sponges. These pieces join together to form a tube-like shape full of small holes that looks like . . . a sponge!

Hard, spiny skin protects a starfish. Hard shells protect the soft bodies of clams and snails. Although scientists group squids with clams and snails, a squid's shell is just a small hard surface inside its head.

What information on this page is interesting but unimportant? Explain.

Many other invertebrates have skeletons that cover the outside of their bodies like plates of armor. Crabs, spiders, and bees all have outside skeletons. Scientists group these animals together because they have legs with joints that help them to walk, swim, or jump. Scientists then divide them into subgroups based on how many legs they have. Bees, like all insects, have six legs. Spiders have eight legs. Crabs have many legs and also two sets of feelers on their heads. They use these feelers to touch things.

Who Knew?

A starfish's stomach can reach into a clam's shell and release juices to digest the clam.

Vertebrates

Vertebrates are animals with backbones. The backbone holds up the skeleton inside the animal's body. This means that these animals can grow very large and still be able to move around well. Backbones also help animals develop large brains. Vertebrates are divided into fish, amphibians, reptiles, birds, and mammals.

> What is important to remember about backbones?

Fish Fish were the first animals on Earth to have

backbones. Many fish have skeletons that are made of bone. Others, like sharks, have skeletons made of a rubbery material. Fins help fish swim through the water. Gills help them breathe in it. Some fish have tiny balloon-like objects inside of them. These objects fill with air to help the fish float.

Amphibians Amphibians were the first animals with

backbones to move onto land from the ocean. Moist skin covers their skeletons. Frogs and toads are examples of amphibians. They have powerful back legs. Other amphibians have four legs of equal size. Some have no legs at all. Most amphibians lay their eggs in water. Their babies live in the water and breathe with gills. As they grow up, they develop lungs to breathe air. Eventually, they move onto land.

Reptiles  Like fish and amphibians, reptiles are cold-blooded vertebrates. To stay warm, they lie out in the sun. Crocodiles, snakes, and lizards are examples of reptiles. They all have dry, scaly skin to protect them. Turtles are also reptiles. They protect their bodies with a bony shell. A few reptiles give birth to live babies. Most, however, lay eggs with tough, waterproof shells.

Birds  Birds are warm-blooded vertebrates. Their feathers keep heat inside their bodies. Instead of arms, birds have wings with which many of them fly. Hollow bones make birds light. This helps them fly. Different birds have different kinds of wings, beaks, and feet, depending on where they live and what they eat.

Mammals  Mammals include humans and most large land animals. Mammals are different from other vertebrates for two reasons. First, most mammals have some sort of hair. Second, mammal mothers feed their young with milk. Most mammals give birth to live babies.

What information is important on this page? Explain your decision.

Who Knew?

The **tuatara** is the last member of a group of reptiles that have lived on Earth since before dinosaurs lived!

Think and Respond

Reflect and Write

- You and your partner have read sections of *Animals*. Discuss what you and your partner retold.

- On index cards, write down one idea you had in response to an important and an unimportant detail of the story. On the back of the index cards, explain your decisions.

Nouns in Context

Reread *Animals* to find examples of nouns. Write down the nouns you find, and then share them with a partner. Work together to write a paragraph about invertebrate and vertebrate animals using the nouns you found.

Turn and Talk

DETERMINE IMPORTANCE

Discuss with a partner what have you learned so far about determining importance.

- How does finding the main ideas and supporting details help you determine importance?

- How does determining importance make you a better reader?

Find one important and one unimportant detail in *Animals*. Explain to a partner why each detail is important or unimportant.

Critical Thinking

In a small group, discuss what characteristics all animals share. Look back at *Animals*. Write down the main differences between invertebrates and vertebrates. Then write answers to these questions.

- How are fish and reptiles different?

- How are birds and mammals different?

- How does this encyclopedia entry support the idea that every animal can be classified?

Contents

Modeled Reading

Memoir Century Farm: 100 Years on a Family Farm
by Cris Peterson 98

Vocabulary
require, pollinate, equipment, reproduction, century 100

Comprehension Strategy !
Create Images 102

Shared Reading

Realistic Fiction Mrs. McClary's Very Weird Garden
by David Dreier 104

Grammar
Proper Nouns 106

Interactive Reading

Observation Log Waking Up a Bean
by Darlene Stille 108

Vocabulary
criteria, conditions, germinate, cones, adapt 114

Poem "Ode to the Giant Redwood" by Tisha Hamilton 116

Word Study
Reference Materials 118

Fairy Tale The Pea Blossom
retold by Ernestine Geisecke 120

Seeds, Fruits, and Flowers

Century Farm

100 Years on a Family Farm

by Cris Peterson   photographs by Alvis Upitis

Appreciative Listening

Appreciative listening is listening for language that helps you create a picture in your mind. Listen to the focus questions your teacher will read to you.

Ask Farmer Joe

Q: I grow apples and pears. I've heard that some farmers set up beehives near their trees. Are beehives a good idea, and will I need a lot of **equipment**?

A: Bees are a good idea—they carry pollen from plant to plant. This helps to **pollinate** many crops including fruit trees. You will need some special equipment, particularly if you want to collect the honey.

Q: My family farm will soon turn 100. How can I have it honored as a farm that is a **century** old?

A: You can have your farm honored through the state's Century Farm Program. The state will **require** you to prove that your family has owned the farm for 100 years or more. You will also need to prove that you are related to the farm's original owner.

Q: Our potatoes were very tasty this year. How can we get that same great taste next year?

A: You are in luck. In the **reproduction** of potatoes, new plants are grown from parent plants.

Structured Vocabulary Discussion

When your teacher says a vocabulary word, have the people in your group take turns saying the first word they think of. Continue until your teacher says, "Stop." Then have the last person who said a word explain how the word is related to the vocabulary word.

Throughout the week, add to your vocabulary journal entries. Record new insights and other words that relate to this week's vocabulary.

Picture It

Copy this word organizer into your vocabulary journal. Fill in the space with kinds of **equipment**.

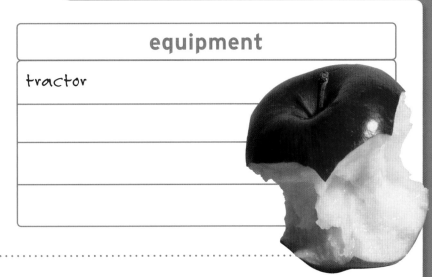

equipment
tractor

Copy this word organizer into your vocabulary journal. Fill in the left arrow with things that are younger than a **century**. Fill in the right arrow with things that are older than a **century**.

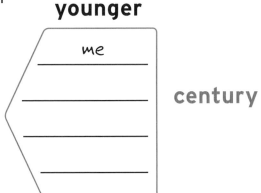

younger

me

century

older

mountains

Comprehension Strategy

Create Images

Creating images is like playing a movie in your mind as you read. Mental images can help you understand and remember what you read. As you read, use the selection's pictures along with your memories and five senses to create images. After you read, think and talk about the images you created.

Create mental IMAGES as you read.

Think about how something you read might look, sound, feel, smell, and taste to create a mental image.

TURN AND TALK Listen as your teacher reads the following lines from *Century Farm*. Then, with your partner, discuss the following questions.

- If you could draw a picture of this farm, what would it look like?
- How do the words make you feel?

I know a farm that is almost as old as dirt. It's a century farm—one hundred years old.

The barn is old. The house is old. The granary is old.

The people who built the farm have died. The first cows and chickens and sheep are all gone.

One hundred years is a long time. . . .

But the old farm is still alive. Young cows graze in the pasture. Young crops in the fields reach for the sun. Young kittens totter around on hay bales in the hayloft. And young kids still care for their cattle in the old barn.

TAKE IT WITH YOU Creating images in your mind when you read is fun. As you read other selections, write down which senses and memories you used to create images. Use a chart like the one below to record your images.

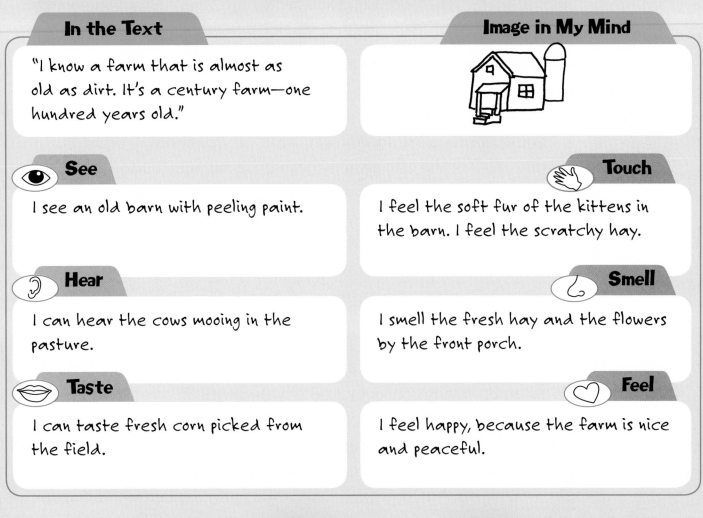

In the Text

"I know a farm that is almost as old as dirt. It's a century farm—one hundred years old."

Image in My Mind

See

I see an old barn with peeling paint.

Touch

I feel the soft fur of the kittens in the barn. I feel the scratchy hay.

Hear

I can hear the cows mooing in the pasture.

Smell

I smell the fresh hay and the flowers by the front porch.

Taste

I can taste fresh corn picked from the field.

Feel

I feel happy, because the farm is nice and peaceful.

Mrs. McClary's Very Weird Garden

by David Dreier

Amelia Salazar walked around the backyard of her new house, smiling. Suddenly her smile disappeared. "What is that *smell*?" she exclaimed, perhaps a bit too loudly.

A cheerful-looking woman popped her head above the low fence between the yards. "I couldn't help hearing you," she said. "I'm Donna McClary."

"Amelia Salazar," Amelia said. "I'm sorry if I disturbed you. But something in my yard smells just awful. Sort of like rotting meat."

Donna McClary laughed. "That smell is coming from *my* yard, not yours. It's my dragon lily," Mrs. McClary said. "Come on over and I'll show you."

Mrs. McClary led Amelia to a group of plants. The plants had beautiful, wide, purplish-red flowers. But the *smell*—it was even stronger here. Seeing the puzzled look on Amelia's face, Mrs. McClary explained, "Dragon lilies need to be pollinated by flies to reproduce. So the lily creates a smell like rotting meat to attract flies."

Amelia was amazed. "But why do want such a stinky plant in your backyard?" she asked.

"I'm the president of the local chapter of the International Carnivorous Plant Society," Mrs. McClary replied. "Do you know anything about carnivorous plants?"

Amelia shook her head no.

"They're plants that eat insects. The dragon lily isn't actually a meat eater. But the Venus flytrap"—she pointed to her t-shirt, which had a picture of a Venus flytrap chomping down on a big juicy fly—"it's a meat eater for sure."

"Meat-eating plants are from areas where there aren't enough nutrients in the soil. So the plants develop ways to trap insects for food. Take my sundew. It traps insects with little sticky hairs on its leaves. It's a plant-eat-bug world in my garden," Mrs. McClary said with a chuckle.

Just then a fly landed on a scary-looking sundew. Its legs became trapped in goo. Mrs. McClary smiled. "Lunch time!" she said.

UNITED STATES BOTANIC Garden

The United States Botanic Garden welcomes you! The garden was established by Congress in 1820. The grounds are home to some 26,000 plants. Come see what we have to offer.

The Conservatory is open from 10 A.M. to 5 P.M. daily. The main gate is at 100 Maryland Avenue. The Conservatory has some 4,000 plants on display. Come see them all. Maybe you want to learn more about plants. We hold lectures and workshops throughout the year. Contact Anna Davis for details.

Bartholdi Park is open from dawn to dusk. Come enjoy the beautiful Bartholdi Fountain. Walk through the outdoor gardens. You can enter the park from Independence Avenue, Washington Avenue, or First Street.

If you are having trouble finding us, look for the Capitol building. We are just down the street. Enjoy your visit!

Proper Nouns

Activity One

About Proper Nouns

A proper noun names a specific person, place, or thing. Your name is a proper noun, and so is the name of the street where you live. The name of your school is also a proper noun. The first letter of a word that is a proper noun is capitalized.

Proper Nouns in Context

With a partner, reread the brochure. Make a list of all the proper nouns you find and write them in a chart like the one below. Be sure to put them under the correct heading.

PERSON	PLACE	THING
	Washington, D.C.	Bartholdi Fountain

Activity Two

Explore Words Together

With a partner, look at the list of words on the right.
Which of these words are proper nouns? Copy the list onto paper and circle the proper nouns. Discuss ways to make all words proper nouns.

Main Street	park
avenue	Senate
Park School	senator

Activity Three

Explore Words in Writing

Choose three of the words on the list above that are NOT proper nouns. Think of a proper noun that relates to each of the three words. Use each word and its proper noun together in a sentence. Share your favorite sentence with a partner.

Waking Up a Bean

by Darlene Stille

March 5

Today my mother and I shopped for beans at the grocery store. The beans are for a science experiment on how plants grow. Beans that we eat are also seeds. I know this because I looked up beans in an encyclopedia. I also looked for information in the Farmers' Almanac. In my experiment, I will test what a seed needs to germinate, or begin growing.

The store had lots of different kinds of dried beans. I chose red kidney beans. I like their shape and their reddish-brown color. Kidney beans are also good for experiments. The beans grow fairly quickly. I'm really excited about this experiment. I'm a little nervous, too. I have never done an experiment on my own before.

Why are fast-growing plants best for student science experiments?

March 6

I counted out 20 kidney beans. My teacher, Ms. Thomas, said to think of a seed as being asleep before it begins to grow. Germinating, or sprouting, is kind of like waking up. The conditions that I will test for waking up seeds are light, moisture, and temperature.

I dropped five dry bean seeds into a plastic storage bag. I set those seeds on the kitchen counter near a window. I wrapped the other 15 seeds in moist paper towels. I put five towel-wrapped seeds into each of three plastic storage bags. I set one bag of seeds on a warm, sunny windowsill. I slid another bag into a dark kitchen drawer. The third bag of seeds I placed on a shelf in the refrigerator.

What mental images do you have about the bean experiment so far?

Two-Word Technique Write down two words that reflect your thoughts about each page. Discuss them with your partner.

March 7

Nothing has happened with the beans in any of the plastic storage bags. So I watched my mother soak the rest of the kidney beans so she could use them in a bean salad. Most people soak beans before cooking them because they have a hard coating. The coating keeps the seed from germinating until conditions are right for the plant to grow. The plant must have the proper conditions of light, water, soil, and temperature in order to grow. This is why seeds only germinate at certain times of the year.

March 8

Still no action in any of the bags. The beans my mother soaked overnight, however, are now soft. I took this chance to see what lies under the seed coating. I peeled the coat off one of the soaked kidney beans. Underneath, the bean had the same shape, but it was white. It also had two halves. I gently pulled the halves apart with my thumbnail. I could see the part that would grow into a new plant and the part that would provide food for the germinating seed.

What memories do you have of growing plants, such as bean seeds?

March 9

I'm so excited! Some of the seeds have started to germinate. Ten bean seeds have split open. All of the seeds that germinated are on moist paper towels—five in sunlight and five in the dark kitchen drawer. What looks like a tiny tail sprouts out of each germinating seed. Part of the seed will grow downward to become the plant's roots. Another part of the seed will reach upward to become the plant stem. The dry seeds and the seeds in the refrigerator have not germinated.

> Describe what another sprouting seed might look like as it grows roots and a stem.

March 10

The sprouts from the 10 seeds grow longer. Once seeds have begun to sprout, they are no longer called "seeds." They are called "seedlings." Seedlings must be planted in soil in order to keep growing.

March 11

The first part of my experiment is complete. I filled out my lab sheet and wrote a report that sums up my findings. I began with seeds that were sleeping. I observed the seeds under different conditions to find out what a seed needs in order to wake up and germinate. None of the dry seeds or the seeds in the refrigerator germinated. The seeds on the window sill and in the drawer germinated. These seeds were wrapped in moist paper towels. I concluded that kidney bean seeds need water and warmth to sprout. The seeds do not need light.

What do seeds need in order to germinate?

Summary of Experiment

March 5: I buy kidney beans

March 6: I start my experiment

March 7: Mother soaks the leftover beans to eat

March 8: I look inside a water-softened bean

March 9: The seeds begin to germinate

March 10: The seeds become seedlings

March 11: I learn what conditions a bean seeds need to germinate

Think and Respond

Reflect and Write

- You and your partner have read *Waking Up a Bean*. Discuss with your partner the words you wrote down.

- Choose two of the words that you discussed. On one side of an index card, write the word. On the other side, write sentences that explain how the word helped you create images.

Proper Nouns in Context

Reread *Waking Up a Bean* to find examples of proper nouns. Write down the words you find. Look for additional words that could be replaced by proper nouns. For example, the *store* could be replaced with *Grover's Market*. List examples of proper nouns for each of these words you find. Share your list with a partner.

Turn and Talk

CREATE IMAGES

Discuss with a partner what you have learned so far about how to create images.

- What does it mean to create images?

- How do you create mental images as you read?

Choose one of the images that you created while reading *Waking up a Bean*. Explain to a partner how that image helped you enjoy and understand the observation log.

Critical Thinking

With a partner, talk about what seeds need to grow. Write your ideas down in a list. Look back over *Waking Up a Bean*. Compare your list with the growing conditions that the authors lists. Then answer these questions.

- What growing conditions are needed for beans to grow successfully?

- How does this observation log support the idea that plants have certain characteristics that help them survive and reproduce?

Conifers

OUR OLDEST PLANTS

Conifers are among the oldest plants on Earth. There are many types of conifers, such as pine trees, spruce trees, and fir trees. All conifers have two **criteria** in common. They are woody plants and they carry their seeds and pollen in **cones**.

Did You Know?

Conifers need the wind to reproduce. Pollen from the male cones is carried by the wind to the female cones. Inside the female cone, the pollen will **germinate**. The pollen tube grows inside the female cone until it reaches the egg. Then the two fuse together to make a new plant.

Conifers: Survivors!

Conifers make up 30 percent of the world's forests. Conifers can survive in harsh **conditions**. Needles help conifers **adapt** to weather. The tiny needles lose less water than flat leaves in hot, dry weather. Needles also do not hold heavy loads of snow that could break branches.

Structured Vocabulary Discussion

Work with a partner to review your vocabulary words. Then classify the words into two groups. Place words that are things in one group. Place words that are actions in the other group. Then share your ideas with the class. Be sure to explain why you placed each word in the group that you did.

Throughout the week, add to your vocabulary journal entries. Record new insights and other words that relate to this week's vocabulary.

Picture It

Copy this word organizer into your vocabulary journal. Fill in the circles with some of the **conditions** in which conifers can survive.

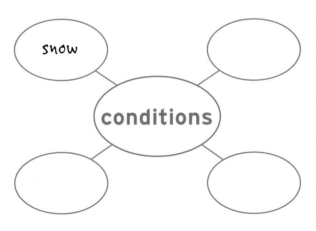

Copy this word organizer into your vocabulary journal. Fill in the table with things that you can do to **adapt** to cold weather.

adapt
put on coat

ODE TO THE GIANT REDWOOD

by Tisha Hamilton

An army of giants as far as I can see.

Silent, proud soldier never able to break free.

With strong, thick arms stretched so high,

You brush your rough hands against the sky.

For centuries you've towered evergreen.

If you could speak! What battles you've seen!

Born from a seed hidden deep in cones.

Once all you saw was earth and stones.

Your oldest enemy, fire, tried to take you away,

Yet somehow you managed to stand and stay.

Even when foes carved holes in your base,

Your thick brown boots held you firmly in place.

You've faced many an enemy's axe; yet you survive.

You know your great size has kept you alive.

Your strong soldier's body and soaring green crown

Are far too amazing to ever be cut down.

Large, ancient, silent, calm, wise, and strong,

You are a brave soldier; you deserve to live long.

Word Study

Alien Invaders!

Profile   Settings   Community   Help

Jake Allen: Alien Invaders! This sounded like a cool research project until I figured out our teacher meant plant invaders. I don't even know where to begin. Help!!!

Lao Vu: Hey, don't panic. I found a list of the 20 "Most Wanted" invaders in my science almanac. There are lots of plants on the list. That will give us a start. We can also look in an encyclopedia. That should give us some more information.

Jake Allen: Don't forget to save the names of your sources for our bibliography. I'll have my mother help me check on the Internet for some good Web sites.

Lao Vu: I found the right encyclopedia article, but I can't get through the first sentence. I didn't even know what non-indigenous meant! Here's what I found in an online dictionary:

non-in•dig•e•nous \non-in-ˈdijə-nəs\ *adj* Not occurring naturally in an area.

Jake Allen: I found this great Web site, but it keeps talking about plants in South Africa. Where is that? I guess I'll have to look up South Africa in an atlas. I think it's going to be a long afternoon!

Share

Buddy Info

Reference Materials

Activity One

About Reference Materials

Reference materials are sources that provide information. When you do a research project, you can use reference materials to find dates, definitions and other important facts. Encyclopedias provide information about many topics. Atlases show geographical facts and maps. Dictionaries tell the meanings of words as well as the pronunciation, part of speech, and origin of the word. Almanacs usually come out each year and give facts about many subjects.

Reference Materials in Context

With a small group, reread Jake's and Lao's message exchange. Find the names of the reference materials in the passage and write them in the correct category in the chart.

INFORMATION ABOUT LOCATIONS	INFORMATION ABOUT WORDS	INFORMATION ABOUT TOPICS
		encyclopedia

Activity Two

Explore Words Together

Look at the list of words on the right. Work with a partner to determine what type of information you are most likely to find in each source. Create a list for each type of reference material. Share your list with the class.

almanac	encyclopedia
atlas	Internet
dictionary	bibliography

Activity Three

Explore Words in Writing

Choose one of the types of reference materials from the list. Use that source to research something about seeds, fruits, or flowers. Then use your research to write a paragraph. Share your paragraph with a partner.

The Pea Blossom

retold by Ernestine Geisecke

Once upon a time, in a secret Persian garden, there were five peas in a single pod. The pod was green, and the peas were green, so the peas decided that the entire world was green.

As the weeks passed, the pod turned brown and the peas turned brown. Obviously, the peas proclaimed, the world had now turned brown.

The peas often wondered what life was like outside the pod. Surely, some adventure must await them.

Then one day, "CRACK! The pod suddenly burst open and the five peas tumbled into a young boy's hand.

"Excellent!" the boy exclaimed, "these peas are perfect for my new pea shooter." He slipped a pea into the shooter, puffed into it, and sent the pea in a high arch across the garden.

"Whee, I'm flying!" shouted the pea. "Catch me if you can!"

The boy shot a second pea high into the air. "I'm headed for the moon!" shouted the pea.

> Why did the peas think the color of the world had changed?

When their turn came, peas three and four proudly announced, "We're on our way to faraway castles to dine among kings and queens!" One pea remained. "Whatever is supposed to happen will happen!" it thought as the boy shot it into the air. The fifth pea tumbled into a window box outside a tiny house, settling into the soft, warm moss.

The house belonged to a woodsman and his frail, delicate daughter. Every day, the woodsman gathered camel-thorn branches to sell as firewood. Although he worked very hard, he seldom had enough money for the two of them.

One morning, as the father prepared for work, the sun shone through the window, across the floor, and onto the girl's bed. The frail girl looked toward the window.

"What is that green thing peeping in the window?" she asked. Her father looked out the window. "Oh, it's a little plant! I wonder how it got here," he replied.

He pushed the girl's bed toward the window so she could see the tiny plant. "Please, Father, would you bring me some books so I can learn about this plant?"

Why do you think the girl wants to learn about the plant?

"Of course, my dear." Later that day, on his way home, he visited the town's wisest, oldest woman. "Madam," he asked, "have you any reference books about plants?"

Say Something Technique Listen as your partner reads part of the text aloud. Choose a point in the text to stop your partner and ask what he or she is thinking about the text at that moment. Then switch roles with your partner.

"Why yes, yes I do," she responded. "Here are books about seeds, fruits, and flowers. And this farmer's almanac gives the criteria for growing healthy plants."

When the father arrived home, his daughter reached for the books. "Oh, thank you, Father. Now I can learn about our little plant."

The next day, she scanned each book, checked each index, and read each table of contents. When her father came home she announced, "Father, our plant is a sweet pea—I'm certain it is." She pointed to a picture in one of the books.

Her father looked at the plant, and then at the picture. "Yes, it does look like a sweet pea. What else did you discover?" He asked not only because he was interested in his daughter, but also because—although he was honorable and hard working—he had never learned how to read. He had started working when he was very young and had never gone to school.

How was the girl able to identify that the plant was a sweet pea?

"Well, because plants developed flowers, they can live and reproduce in many different environments," replied the girl. "Some plants, like this one, live only one year. These plants adapt by using all their energy to produce flowers which then form pods filled with seeds for next year's plants."

"How interesting." Her father looked at the plant and then at his daughter. He thought that as the pea plant grew taller, his daughter grew stronger. But he could not be certain.

A few days later he inquired, "What has happened to the little plant?"

His daughter reached toward the plant. "Oh, Father, it has developed beautiful blossoms and a truly wonderful aroma."

The old man agreed as he looked from the plant to his daughter, and again to the plant. Could it be that as the plant grew colorful, the color returned to his daughter's cheeks? He could not be certain; perhaps his hopes were fooling his eyes.

Why does the father think the plant is extraordinary?

Another week passed. Now the old man became convinced that the plant was truly extraordinary. He sat at the corner of his daughter's bed. "Tell me about the plant," he whispered.

"The weather's been unusually sunny and warm. The plant has grown quite tall, and its blossoms are huge. So huge that it needs help to stand. I placed this camel-thorn branch here in the window box to hold up the plant and its blossoms to the sun."

The father wept tears of joy. It was not his imagination! Indeed, as the pea blossom had grown taller, his daughter had grown stronger. Now, the plant's lovely blossoms and sweet aroma strengthened both their lives.

And what happened to the other peas? The pea that yearned to fly was eaten by a peacock and now flies about the garden. The pea that wished for the moon was eaten by a cow, and we know the cow's horns are the shape of the crescent moon. And the peas that boasted of knowing kings and queens? They fell into a bowl of raisins and dates set before the prince.

But the pea who believed, "Whatever is supposed to happen will happen!" grew and thrived in the window box. This pea formed blossoms, bore fruit, and produced seeds so there would be many little children of the pea blossom to come.

What point do you think the author is trying to make about the other peas?

Think and Respond

Reflect and Write

- You and your partner have read sections of *The Pea Blossom*. Discuss the thoughts you and your partner had when you read the text.

- Choose two inferences you made. On one side of an index card write the section you read. On the other side of the index card, write the inference. Then look for a set of partners who read different sections. Discuss the sections you read and the inferences you were able to make.

Reference Materials in Context

Reread *The Pea Blossom* to find examples of reference materials. Then work with a partner to look up interesting facts about peas in each of these references. Use the information you find to write a paragraph about peas. Share your paragraph with the class.

Turn and Talk

INFER

Discuss with a partner what you have learned so far about what it means to infer.

- What is an inference based on? How can making inferences help you understand what you read?

Choose one of inferences you made while reading *The Pea Blossom*. Discuss with a partner how you made the inference and how it helped you better understand the story.

Critical Thinking

In a small group, talk about what you already know about fairy tales. Make a list of the characteristics of a fairy tale. Look back at *The Pea Blossom*. Discuss what happened to the fifth pea and how its fate was different from that of the other peas. Then answer these questions.

- What did each pea say, and what happened to each pea?

- How did the fifth pea change the life of the woodsman and his daughter?

- What do you think the author intended as the moral or message of this story?

Tornado Over Kansas, 1929
John Steuart Curry (1897–1946)

UNIT: Across the U.S.A.

THEME **5** One Country, Many Regions

THEME **6** The Land Shapes People's Lives

Viewing

The artist who painted this picture was John Steuart Curry. He liked to paint pictures of life on the prairies of the Midwest. He painted this picture of a Kansas farm family in 1929.

1. What can you tell about the geography of the region from this painting?

2. What can you tell about the climate of the region from the painting?

3. How do you think the people's lives are affected by living in the region shown in the painting?

In This UNIT

In this unit, you will read about the geography and climate of different parts of the United States. You will also explore how the land shapes people's lives.

Contents

Modeled Reading

Adventure Fire Storm by Jean Craighead George.................130

Vocabulary
canyon, region, surround, solution, dense 132

Comprehension Strategy ❗
Use Fix-Up Strategies..134

Shared Reading

Personal Narrative The Superstition Mountains
by Bradley Hannan..136

Word Study
Synonyms and Antonyms 138

Interactive Reading

Fantasy Who Believes in Buried Treasure?
by Jeanie Stewart 140

Vocabulary
aspect, impact, alter, climate, plateau.............................146

Song "This Land Is Your Land" by Woodie Guthrie..............148

Word Study
Multiple-Meaning Words 150

Expository Take a Virtual Trip by Alice McGinty.................152

One Country, Many Regions

FIRESTORM

by Jean Craighead George

illustrated by Wendell Minor

Precise Listening

Precise listening is listening for special word meanings. Listen to the focus questions your teacher will read to you.

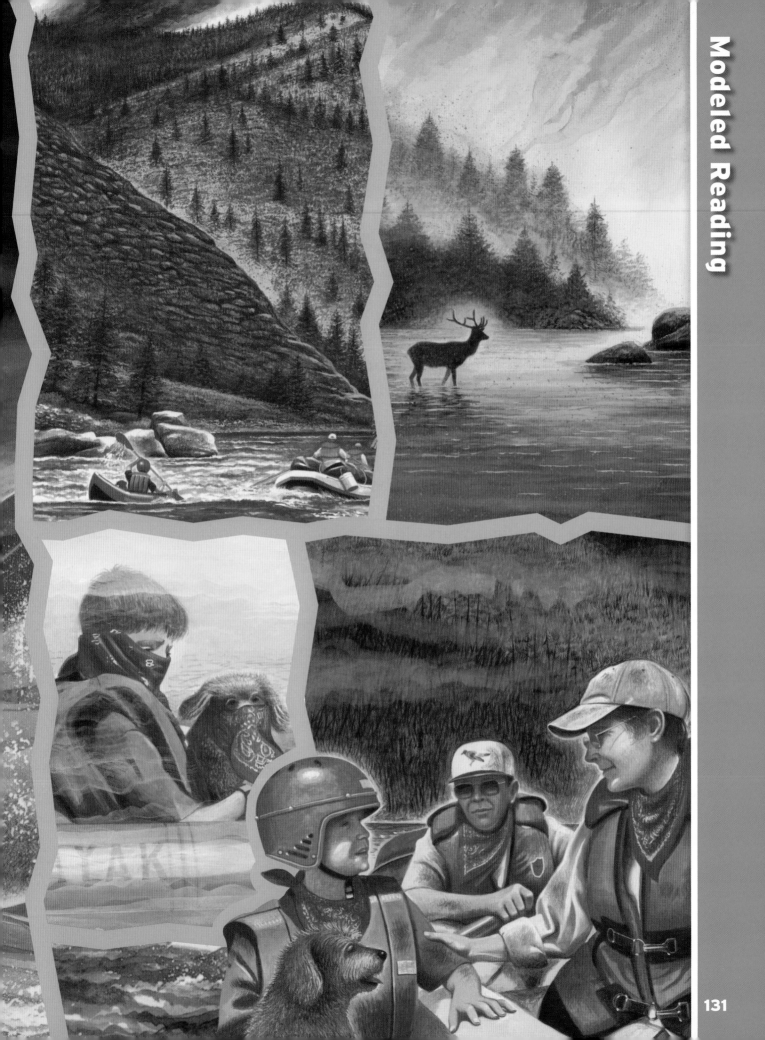

IDAHO'S SALMON RIVER

River Facts

- The Salmon River is also called the "River of No Return." The name comes from the power of its swift waters. Lewis and Clark explored the **region** in the early 1800s. They quickly learned that their canoes were no match for the river!

- For many years, boats could travel only downriver. Powerboats brought the **solution** for two-way trips.

- The Salmon River runs through a very deep **canyon**. It is even deeper than the Grand Canyon! The rock in the canyon walls may be 1.5 billion years old.

- The Salmon was once named the Lewis River. Its name was changed when people discovered that it was **dense** with salmon.

- Miners flocked to Idaho when gold was discovered in the early 1860s. Tents soon covered the lands that **surround** the river.

canyon   region   surround   solution   dense

Structured Vocabulary Discussion

Work with a partner to fill in the following blanks with the correct word from the box above. Be sure you can explain how the words are related.

Acre is to *farm* as _____ is to *country*.

Region is to *area* as *thick* is to _____.

Solution is to *answer* as *enclose* is to _____.

Hill is to *mountain* as *hole* is to _____.

Throughout the week, add to your vocabulary journal entries. Record new insights and other words that relate to this week's vocabulary.

Picture It

Copy the word web into your vocabulary journal. Fill in the empty circles with things that can **surround** something.

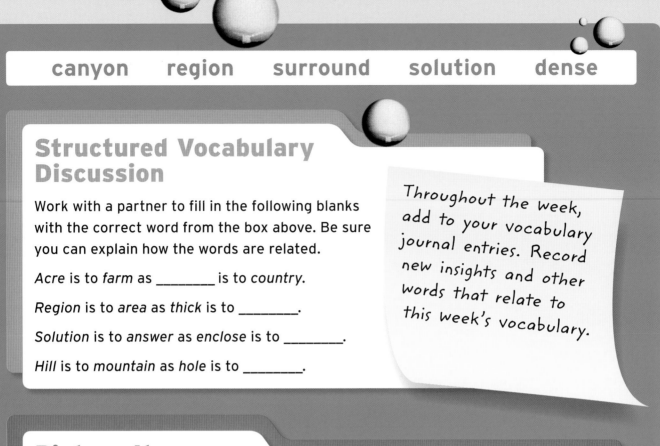

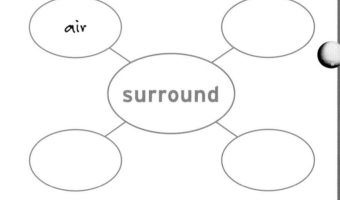

Use a chart like this one below. Put words that mean the same as **dense** in the left column. Put words that mean the opposite in the right column.

dense	
same	**opposite**
thick	thin

133

Use Fix-Up Strategies

Using fix-up strategies is a way to solve problems when you read. Some fix-up strategies are reading on for meaning or using illustrations, phonics, or word attack skills.

FIX-UP STRATEGIES help when you get stuck on a word.

Stuck on Word → Word Attack

When you get stuck on a word, try different strategies to help you figure it out.

TURN AND TALK Listen as your teacher reads the following lines from *Fire Storm*. With a partner, discuss any difficulties you had in understanding the story. Use fix-up strategies to help you solve any problems with the text.

• Think about the meaning of *fluorescent*. Can you read the passage without stopping to find out the meaning of the word?

• What other fix-up strategy could you use to help you continue reading and understanding?

The next morning the sun shone through the dense smoke and colored the river, the boats, and the people a strange fluorescent orange. It was cold. Bandanas over their faces, their eyes watering, the little party cheered when the sun climbed higher. The air cleared, and they could see the river. They pushed off into the charred wilderness.

As Axel passed miles of smoldering trees and smoking stumps, he grew terribly sad. He paddled up to Uncle Paul and Aunt Charlotte's raft and clung to it.

TAKE IT WITH YOU Using fix-up strategies will help you understand what you read. As you read other selections, determine the problems you face and choose the appropriate fix-up strategy. Use a chart like the one below to help you with the process.

Word I Got Stuck On	What I Did				Which One Worked?
	Used Illustrations	Used Phonics	Read On	Broke It into Parts	
fluorescent	✓	✓	✔	✓	Read On

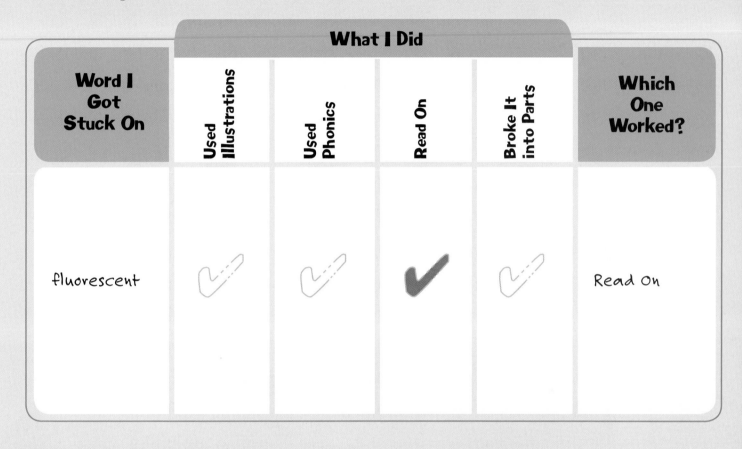

The Superstition Mountains

by Bradley Hannan

*M*y family moved from Pennsylvania to Phoenix, Arizona, last spring. It's so different here! Our new neighbor, Mr. Ramírez, suggested that we visit the Superstition Mountains east of town. That would give us an idea of just how different Arizona is from my old home.

"The Superstition Mountains? What are those?" my brother Steve and I wondered. Would they be scary? We wanted to know before we went. So we asked our Aunt Helen. She had taught school in Apache Junction, a town close to the mountains. We figured she would know all about them.

She told us that the mountains are a group of peaks, cliffs, and mesas. There isn't a single summit, even though people sometimes talk about Superstition Mountain. The mountains are located on the edge of a vast wilderness area. She said there is also a great state park at the base of the mountains—the Lost Dutchman State Park. It is a very popular place to hike.

Aunt Helen wasn't interested in hiking, though. She liked the legends. People claim gold is hidden in the mountains. The story is that Jacob Waltz mined there in the late 1800s. Although he was a German immigrant, people called him "The Dutchman." People say he got lucky. He was always paying for things with gold nuggets. But he died without revealing the mine's location. Even to this day, people still search for the Lost Dutchman Mine!

We went to see the Superstition Mountains and the Lost Dutchman State Park. The mountains were so huge that I felt tiny. We even took a drive along the Apache Trail. It was beautiful. Mr. Ramírez was right—visiting Superstition Mountain did help us appreciate how different our new home is. We love Arizona.

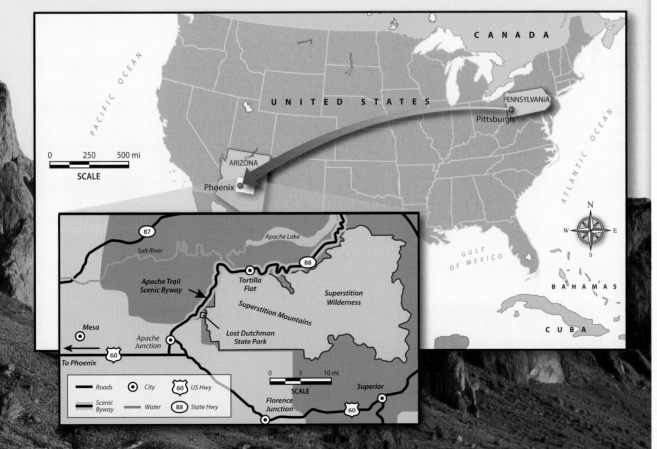

Word Study

Our Vacation to Tonto National Monument

We had a great time at Tonto. It's in Arizona. We saw cliff houses built by the Salado people around 700 years ago! Here are some of my favorite memories.

The Salado had to climb a ladder to get to their second story. I would hate to have to ascend and descend ladders all day!

Cacti are growing on the hillside above the monument. If you look down, you can see Salado cliff dwellings underneath a rock ledge.

We visited Tonto soon after a wildfire. It was scary. Fires can quickly spread over vast areas and destroy both tiny plants and huge cacti.

We climbed to the top of a high hill at Tonto. My brother thought all of the people at the bottom looked like ants from the summit! My mom really liked the ancient Salado pottery. Even though it was very old, she thought it looked new.

Synonyms and Antonyms

Activity One

About Synonyms and Antonyms

A synonym is a word that means the same as another word. For example, *loving* is a synonym for *kind*. An antonym is a word that means the opposite of another word. *Unkind* and *cruel* are antonyms for *kind*.

Synonyms and Antonyms in Context

With a partner, look back at *Our Vacation to Tonto National Monument*. Make a list of words that have synonyms and antonyms. Then exchange lists with another set of partners. Copy the chart below and fill it in using the list of words you were given.

WORD	SYNONYM	ANTONYM
cheerful	happy	sad

Activity Two

Explore Words Together

Look at the list of words on the right. With a partner, list a synonym and an antonym for each word.

always	stay
keep	arrive
refuse	noisy

Activity Three

Explore Words in Writing

Choose three of the synonyms or antonyms from the previous activity. Write a short paragraph using each of the words you chose. You might want to try writing sentences to add to captions for the photos on page 138. Share your paragraphs with your partner.

Who Believes in Buried TREASURE?

by Jeanie Stewart

1 groaned and climbed over another rock. I am a city girl who likes malls and museums. So why was I dressed like a coal miner and following my cousin Mateo and my grandmother up a mountain? Because Mateo believes anything anyone tells him, that's why.

Last night Granny told us about a man who buried silver in these mountains three hundred years ago. When Mateo heard that the treasure had never been found, he got excited. He said that he'd peeked into a boarded-up cave on Granny's property yesterday and had seen silver coins.

Granny knew about the cave. She said she'd take us exploring, but only if we did it safely. So, here we were.

"Turn on your lights and follow me," Granny said, after pulling away the boards.

We were hardly inside when Mateo dropped to the ground. "Ana, I told you I saw coins!"

"Some treasure," I said when he held up six quarters. "Now we're each fifty cents richer."

What is Mateo excited about?

"Fine. If you don't want your share, I'll keep it," he said. He dropped the quarters into his pack. Granny grinned. "Let's explore," she said.

Following Granny deeper into the cave, we walked, we crawled, and sometimes we scooted on our bellies like snakes. We got dirty, but it was fun. Twice Granny pointed out coins. When Mateo dusted them off, they were always quarters.

We saw stalagmites and stalactites. It is amazing how tiny drops of water can alter rock. We passed a spring and stopped to rest beside a wall that looked like a frozen waterfall.

> What can context clues tell you about stalagmites and stalactites?

Granny was ready to start back, but Mateo wasn't. He said he saw more coins and squeezed through a crack in the waterfall. Granny said there were no more coins. How could she be so sure? I wondered. When she yelled for Mateo to come back, her only answer was an echo.

"I'd better go after him," she said. "I've never explored back there. It could be dangerous." She tried to squeeze through the crack after Mateo, but even after taking off her pack she wouldn't fit.

Reverse Think-Aloud Technique Listen as your partner reads part of the text aloud. Choose a point in the text to stop your partner and ask what he or she is thinking about the text at that moment. Then switch roles with your partner.

It was up to me to bring my cousin back. When I squeezed through the opening, I could barely see Mateo's light bobbing in the distance. I hurried after him. Finally, when he stopped to pick up something, I caught up with him.

"I found more coins," Mateo said excitedly. "They're not quarters either—they're really old currency!" He showed me.

"Great, but we have to go back," I said.

Mateo dropped the coins into his pack. "I'm not going back without the treasure," he said stubbornly.

He took off with me so close behind him that when he stopped suddenly, I crashed into him. The impact sent us falling over the edge. Suddenly we were sliding and tumbling down a chute like one at our waterpark—but without the water.

What is a *chute*? What fix-up strategies would help you if you did not know the meaning?

Mateo and I landed with a hard thud. In front of us was a narrow tunnel with a small circle of light at the end. "I think we've found another way out of the cave," I said.

We scooted through the tunnel and climbed out into the sunshine. Everything seemed different somehow.

Not far away I heard voices. Mateo grabbed me and shoved me back into the hole.

"Shhh!" he said.

We crouched in the dirt and peeked out as two men stopped beside the hole.

They looked like they belonged in a book about the American Revolution. Their accents were odd. They were griping about the government and the king.

But the United States doesn't have a king!

One of the men grumbled that he should be able to make his own money with his own silver. The other man called him Powell and warned him about being caught.

"Powell!" Mateo whispered excitedly. "That's the man who hid the treasure! I think we're back in the 1700s!"

"I think you hit your head too hard back there," I said.

The men shoved a bag of coins into the hole. When they turned back for their other bag, Mateo scooped coins from the first bag into his pack.

The man called Powell poked his head into the hole and shouted that little people with glowing eyes were stealing his silver. We didn't try to explain—we just took off the way we'd come.

They followed. We had a head start, but by the time we got halfway up the chute, they were gaining on us. It took both of us to drag Mateo's heavy pack over the top.

We were almost back to Granny when a rock hit my shoulder. "They're throwing rocks at us!" I said, but my voice was lost in a rumble like thunder.

I shoved my pack ahead of me into the crack of the waterfall wall.

Why does Mateo think he and his cousin are in the 1700s?

143

The rumble got louder and rocks began raining down. The men hadn't been throwing rocks. The ceiling was caving in. Granny grabbed my pack and pulled on my arm, urging me to hurry. I pulled on Mateo, and he pulled on his bulging pack, but it was stuck in the rock wall. Suddenly a huge rock smashed the pack. Mateo's hands slipped free and all three of us tumbled backwards.

What do you think the word *bulging* means? What clues can you find to help you understand the word?

"Keep moving," Granny ordered, giving Mateo a little shove. "Don't stop until you're out of the cave!"

We hurried, but no rocks fell in the front part of the cave. All was quiet, except for Mateo's grumbling about losing his treasure.

"That was quite an adventure, wasn't it?" Granny asked as she nailed the boards back over the cave's entrance.

"Next summer, I'm going back in there and I'm finding my treasure," Mateo said, giving us both a defiant look.

As we started back down the hill, I whispered to Granny, "I know you planted the quarters. But how did you arrange for those strange men to be there?"

"What men?" Granny asked. "Where?"

Hmmm. Had we really gone back to the 1700s?

"I think I'll let Mateo tell you about it when we get back," I said. I knew Mateo believed we had. He'll believe anything.

Think and Respond

Reflect and Write

- You and your partner have read sections of *Who Believes in Buried Treasure?* Discuss the questions you asked and the answers.

- Choose two fix-up strategies you used and write them on index cards. On the back of the card write the problem that the fix-up strategy helped you solve.

Synonyms and Antonyms in Context

Reread *Who Believes in Buried Treasure?* to find examples of synonyms and antonyms. Write down the words you find. Define each word and use it correctly in a sentence. Share your favorite sentence with a partner.

Turn and Talk

USE FIX-UP STRATEGIES

Discuss with a partner what have you learned so far about fix-up strategies.

- What are some examples of fix-up strategies?

- How do you use fix-up strategies?

Choose one problem you had while reading *Who Believes in Buried Treasure?* Explain to a partner how you used a fix-up strategy to solve the problem.

Critical Thinking

With a partner, brainstorm what you know about caves. Then return to *Who Believes in Buried Treasure?* On a sheet of paper, write in one column what you know about caves. In another column write what details about caves you read in the story. Then answer these questions.

- How is the cave that Mateo explores different from what you know about caves? How is it similar?

- What conclusion can you draw about the caves and the region in which Granny lives?

Vocabulary

PEAKS and PLATEAUS:

Hiking the Appalachian Trail

March 13

My family planned to take pictures of wildflowers on our spring break camping trip along the Appalachian Trail in Virginia. A late-season snowfall made us **alter** our plans today. We built a snow fort instead!

March 14

The snow had an **impact** on today's hike. We covered only a mile. We did see some wildflowers, though. A dogtooth violet pushed its head up through the snow.

March 15

The sun came out today. The snow is quickly melting. I think the **climate** is going to turn out to be perfect for hiking.

March 16

Next year I want to go someplace flat on Spring Break! It seemed like the whole hike was uphill today. I was very happy when we finally reached a **plateau**.

March 17

Taking pictures is my favorite **aspect** of the trip. I just missed capturing a bear chasing a young deer. The bear was out enjoying the sun after his long winter's nap.

Structured Vocabulary Discussion

When your teacher says a vocabulary word, your group will take turns saying the first word you think of. After a few seconds, your teacher will say, "Stop." The last person who said a word should explain how that word is related to the vocabulary word your teacher started with.

Throughout the week, add to your vocabulary journal entries. Record new insights and other words that relate to this week's vocabulary.

Picture It

Copy a word circle like this into your vocabulary journal. Fill in the circle with things you can **alter**.

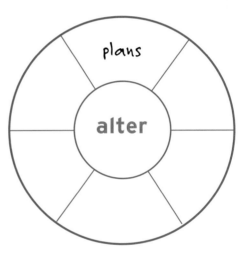

Draw a word web like this in your vocabulary journal. Fill in the empty circles with things that describe **climate**.

147

This LAND is Your LAND

by Woody Guthrie

This land is your land, this land is my land
From the Redwood Forest to the New York Island
The Canadian mountain to the Gulf Stream waters
This land is made for you and me.

As I go walking this ribbon of highway
I see above me this endless skyway
And all around me the wind keeps saying:
"This land is made for you and me."

I roam and I ramble and I follow my footsteps

'Til I come to the sands of her mineral desert

The mist is lifting and the voice is saying:

"This land's made for you and me."

Where the wind's blowing I go a strolling

The wheat field waving and the dust a rolling

The fog's lifting and the wind's saying:

"This land is made for you and me."

Nobody living can ever stop me

As I go walking my freedom highway

Nobody living can make me turn back

This land is made for you and me.

New Drama Series   CHANNEL 8 • SUNDAY

It's Plain to See That "Plain Truth" is a HIT!

Every March, a few new television programs take the place of failed ones. This year I see a home run, "Plain Truth," a show set on the high plains of Texas. This family program has stars that will make you smile through your tears, and great plots and sets that will make the past come alive.

In the late 1860s, the Graysons leave a run-down farm in Mississippi. They trade it for a farm on the high plains of Texas without one tree for miles to block the wind.

Annie Grayson cries at the first sight of her new home made out of sod. Still, thinking back over her old life, usually she can smile.

If Annie has her mind on a cloud, her sister Amanda has her feet on the ground. Together they set out to make the plains their present and their future.

In the first show, the girls tackle the family's water problem. Using a forked stick and faith, they look for a spring. By the end of the show, viewers will line up to help them dig a well.

Multiple-Meaning Words

Activity One

About Multiple-Meaning Words

A multiple-meaning word is a word with more than one meaning. For example, a *show* can mean something we watch, like a television program. The word *show* can be something we do, such as show someone a book. Listen for multiple-meaning words as your teacher reads the television review.

Multiple-Meaning Words in Context

With a partner, read the first paragraph of the review. Make a list of words that have more than one meaning. Then exchange lists with another set of partners. Use the lists to fill in a table like the one below.

WORD	FIRST MEANING	SECOND MEANING
place	to put	an area or space

Activity Two

Explore Words Together

Look at the list on the right. Work with a partner to list the multiple meanings of each word.

leaves	farm
plain	mind
set	cloud

Activity Three

Explore Words in Writing

Choose three multiple-meaning words from the last paragraph of the review. Write three pairs of sentences using two meanings of each word you chose. You might want to try writing sentences to add to the review.

TAKE A VIRTUAL TRIP

by Alice McGinty

Come! Step into a cavern. Climb down a canyon. Walk on the floor of an ancient sea. Take a virtual trip across the United States. You will see landforms that were formed over millions of years. On your journey, you will discover what made the Earth the way it is today.

A Trip to the Great Plains

The first stop on your virtual trip takes you to a wide, flat land. You look out past blowing prairie grass. You can see for miles! You realize you are standing in the Great Plains of Nebraska.

What image comes to your mind when you think of the Great Plains?

Long ago, much of the United States was covered by shallow seas. The sediment from ocean life dropped to the sea floor. Pressure slowly turned the sediment into rock.

You begin to walk across the plain. You are stepping on a sea floor thousands of feet thick. Of course, the seas have been gone for about seventy million years. Since then, other rock has covered the sea floor.

You come to a slow-moving stream. Taking off your shoes, you dip your feet into the cool water. It was streams like this that brought most of the younger rock to the plains. The streams flowed from far away. They carried sediment from distant volcanoes and mountains. As the streams slowed on the flat plains, the sediment settled here.

In other areas of the plains, rocks were brought by glaciers during the ice age. The glaciers picked up rocks and dirt in the north and carried it to the plains. After the ice age, the climate became dry. The sun was so strong that the spruce forests that had grown here died.

What image do the words "ice age" create for you?

Now you sit under a tree by the stream. You feel lucky for the cool shade in the middle of the great open plain.

Rocky Mountains

Great Plains

Colorado Plateau

Appalachian Mountains

A Trip to the Appalachian Mountains

The next stop on your trip takes you to a cavern. You are deep in the Appalachian Mountains of Virginia. When you step into the cavern, you feel a cool dampness from the limestone walls around you. Shivering, you go down a rocky stairway. White stalactites hang from the ceiling. The layers of limestone around you formed millions of years ago. They formed from sediment in the ancient seas, just as with the Great Plains. However, in this area of the country, two plates under the Earth later collided. They pushed the rock up to make mountains. Then water slowly wore away the limestone to make caves.

Two-Word Technique Write down two words that reflect your thoughts about each page. Discuss them with your partner.

How do you think it would feel to be deep in a cavern underground?

Look closely. The layers of limestone that formed one on top of the other are turned on their sides! They are running up and down from floor to ceiling like huge stripes. When the Earth's plates shifted, the rocks folded. You realize that you are walking through a big fold in the Earth.

The Appalachian Mountain chain is the oldest in the United States. Its peaks are not as high as those of other mountain chains. This is because erosion has worn away its surfaces. Rivers and streams have carved out valleys. Standing outside the cavern, you see the sparkle of a waterfall on a mountain. You know that it is slowly changing the face of the Earth.

Stalactites and Stalagmites

A Trip to the Colorado Plateau

You are now on top of an immense cliff. In the distance, other cliffs are carved from the flat, rust-colored rock. Your virtual trip has brought you to a high, flat land west and south of the Rocky Mountains. It is called the Colorado Plateau. The Colorado Plateau takes up parts of the states of Colorado, Utah, New Mexico, and Arizona.

Slowly, you bend to look over the cliff. Your heart pounds as you peer down into the Grand Canyon. Thousands of feet below, through the mist, you see the Colorado River. You know that it was this peaceful looking river that formed these cliffs. It carved out the rocks over the millions of years since it's been flowing.

Why do you think your heart might pound if you looked down into the Grand Canyon?

You follow the narrow trail that leads into the canyon. Holding your breath, you stay close to the rock wall. You pass limestone, sandstone and shale. The minerals in each kind of rock color the cliff wall in shades of red, yellow and green. As you go lower and lower into the canyon, you know you are passing through history. The rocks near the top formed several hundred million years ago. The rocks near the bottom may be up to two thousand million years old!

As you leave the Colorado Plateau, you see the peaks of the Rocky Mountains to the north and east. These mountains are younger and taller than the Appalachian Mountains. The climate in the area is drier, too. Not as much rain has eroded the rugged peaks.

You have finished your virtual trip. Can you see the red dirt of the Grand Canyon on your shoes? Can you remember the chill of the Appalachian cavern? How did it feel to walk on the floor of an ancient sea? Your adventures are not over, though. Think about the landforms that are near your own home. How were they formed? What part of history can you walk though in your own backyard?

What is your favorite image mental image from the virtual trip? Why?

Think and Respond

Reflect and Write

• You and your partner have read *Take a Virtual Trip*. Discuss the words you wrote down.

• Choose two of the words. On one side of an index card, write the word. On the other side, write what image the word brought to mind.

Word Exploration

Reread *Take a Virtual Trip* to find examples of multiple-meaning words. Write down the words you find. Share your list with a partner. Then work together to create graphic organizers that show the multiple meanings of several of the words.

Turn and Talk

CREATE IMAGES

Discuss with a partner what have you learned so far about creating images.

• When and how do you create images?

• How does creating images make you a better reader?

Find two images in *Take a Virtual Trip*. Describe the images to a partner and explain how they helped you better understand what you read.

Critical Thinking

In a group, talk about the climate and geography of each region discussed in *Take a Virtual Trip*. List the regions that are described in the selection. Write the major landforms of each region. Identify any details about climate. Discuss with your group how a region can be defined by its geographic features. Then answer these questions.

• Why is the study of geography important?

• What kinds of information does the study of landforms give you?

Contents

Modeled Reading

Observation Log Arctic Lights, Arctic Nights
by Debbie S. Miller 160

Vocabulary
farmland, fertile, vast, horizon, reflection 162

Comprehension Strategy !
Synthesize 164

Shared Reading

Realistic Fiction My A-Mazing Summer Vacation
by Myka-Lynne Sokoloff 166

Word Study
Homonyms 168

Interactive Reading

Memoir The Gigantic Redwoods: A Memoir
by Mrs. J. B. Rideout retold by M. J. Cosson 170

Vocabulary
access, surroundings, recreation, port, altitude...........176

Photo Essay Key West, Florida by Sue Miller.............178

Grammar
Verbs 180

Historical Fiction Mountain Homestead
by Linda Lott 182

The Land Shapes People's Lives

ARCTIC LIGHTS
by Debbie S. Miller   illustrated by Jon Van Zyle
ARCTIC NIGHTS

Strategic Listening

Strategic listening means listening to make sure you understand the selection. Listen to the focus questions your teacher will read to you.

August 21

November 21

December 21

June 21

Alaska's GIANT Vegetables

John Evans of Palmer, Alaska, holds the record for growing the world's biggest carrot. It weighed almost 19 pounds! Mr. Evans has also grown other huge vegetables. One of his beets weighed almost 43 pounds!

Did You Know?

A lot of sunlight helps Alaskans grow big vegetables. At the height of summer, the sun stays above the **horizon** for more than 17 hours a day!

GIANT VEGETABLES need both sunlight and **fertile** soil to grow so big. Palmer, where Mr. Evans lives, is a town in southern Alaska. It's an area of rich **farmland**. Palmer is also home to the Alaska State Fair. Mr. Evans and other growers bring their vegetables to the fair to compete for awards.

Fun Fact! In 2001, Mr. Evans grew a cabbage that weighed 70 pounds. That was certainly a **reflection** of his gardening skills! Even so, his plant wasn't a record-setter. The biggest cabbage ever raised in the **vast** state of Alaska weighed 106 pounds. Now that's a lot of coleslaw!

Structured Vocabulary Discussion

When your teacher says a vocabulary word, you and your partner should each write all of the words you think of on a piece of paper. When your teacher says, "Stop," share your words with a partner. Take turns explaining to each other the words on your list.

Throughout the week, add to your vocabulary journal entries. Record new insights and other words that relate to this week's vocabulary.

Picture It

Copy this word organizer into your vocabulary journal. Fill in the empty sections with things that are **vast**.

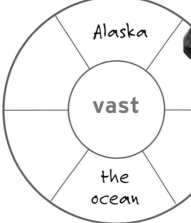

Alaska

vast

the ocean

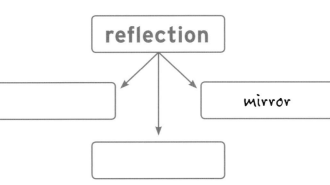

Copy this word organizer into your vocabulary journal. Fill in the blanks with places where you can see your **reflection**.

reflection

mirror

Synthesize

To synthesize means to combine the important ideas in a text. When you synthesize, you put together the important ideas about the overall meaning of a passage and come up with a new insight.

When you SYNTHESIZE, you bring ideas together.

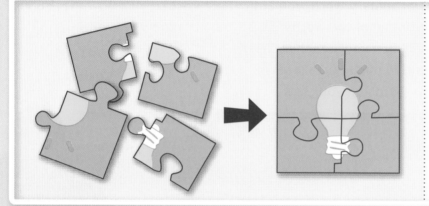

As you read, bring pieces of information together to form a new idea.

TURN AND TALK Listen to your teacher read the following lines from *Arctic Lights, Arctic Nights*. With a partner, discuss the following questions.

• What are the important ideas in the passage?

• What would you tell a friend about what you have read?

Hush . . . silence. Temperatures may fall to 40 degrees below zero. In the twilight, the moose nibble on twigs and bark to survive the winter. As the Alaska-blue sky grows dark, they bed down in the powdery snow.

On winter solstice, the top of the world tilts away from the sun. The nights are long, and the cold runs deep. During the shortest day of the year, a family bundles up and watches nature's holiday celebration. The magical northern lights dance and swirl across the clear, icy sky.

TAKE IT WITH YOU To synthesize, bring the important ideas together for the overall meaning. As you read other selections, use a chart like the one below to help synthesize information.

After Reading I Know That...	This Information Helps Me Understand That...
The temperature may fall to 40 degrees below zero.	Winter in Alaska is very cold and dark. It is also beautiful, because of the northern lights.
On the winter solstice, the top of the world tilts away from the sun.	
You can see the northern lights during the long night.	

My A-mazing Summer Vacation

by Myka-Lynne Sokoloff

Sometimes when you travel to new places, you see things in a different way. Last summer, my mom had to work, so she arranged for me to visit my cousin Tommy. We are the same age, but that's all we have in common. I live in the city, and he's a farm boy growing up in Iowa.

I really didn't want to go to Iowa. Of course, all I knew about Iowa was that the state grew lots and lots of corn, so I assumed I would be completely bored.

I was still grumbling as Mom put me on the plane to my cousin's. My aunt and uncle and cousin all welcomed me and asked what I wanted to do. I wondered if we could go to a park or listen to music. My uncle considered that and replied, "After the chores are done."

My cousin and I got to work. First we gathered eggs from the henhouse; then we cleaned out the horse stalls. We took a break playing in the hayloft before we fed the goats and sheep. My uncle took me on his tractor and let me steer.

I was exhausted after all those chores. Then my uncle announced that Tommy and I had earned a trip to a park to listen to some music.

The park was unlike anything I had experienced before. A farmer had mowed a maze all through his cornfield. We walked around and around on the coarse, bumpy path, trying to find our way out. The corn was so tall we couldn't see which way to go.

That evening, we attended a cornhusking bee. Uncle Tim explained that farmers used to get together to husk corn by hand. They combined the chore with recreation.

We raced to decide the fastest corn husker. Soon a fiddle player started the music, and people started to dance. It was different from the park or music I was used to!

Now I'm home, and I go skateboarding with my friends. Skateboarding is okay when I'm in the city. But I'll leave my board home next time I go to Iowa. I can't wait until I'm old enough to drive that tractor!

Shellfishing in the CHESAPEAKE BAY

11:34 AM

Subject: Hello from Maryland!
From: Danny Osborne
To: Jeff Moore

Hi Jeff,

Yesterday, we went to Chesapeake Bay to collect mussels and blue crabs. Because I was new at collecting shellfish, my aunt and uncle offered their assistance. But I caught on fast to the activity and didn't need two assistants. I didn't say that aloud, though—it would have been rude, and in my family rudeness isn't allowed.

First, we gathered mussels. It sure takes muscles to dig mussels out of the mud! Later, we caught blue crabs from a pier with dipping nets. At the end of the day, I let my aunt and uncle peer into my two sacks to see all the crabs and mussels I had collected.

By then, the tide was going out, so we tied up our sacks and headed back to the house. My aunt made mussel stew and crab cakes for dinner. Everything was delicious. It's hard to find food like that in Wyoming!

That's all for now.

Danny

Homonyms

Activity One

About Homonyms

Homonyms are words that sound the same but have different meanings and spellings. When you hear words such as *weight* and *wait*, you can tell which word is meant by how it is used in the sentence. As your teacher reads Danny's e-mail to Jeff, listen for the homonyms.

Homonyms in Context

With a small group read Danny's e-mail. Find words in his message that are homonyms. Write down each word of the homonym pair, and give the meaning of each word.

HOMONYM	MEANING	HOMONYM	MEANING
aloud	to say out loud	allowed	permitted

Activity Two

Explore Words Together

The list on the right contains words that have homonyms. List the homonym for each word and define it. Then compare your list with a partner.

billed	led
creek	rode
higher	sore

Activity Three

Explore Words in Writing

Choose four homonym pairs from your Activity Two list. Write a short letter on any subject using your homonyms. Put each pair of homonyms as close together in the letter as you can. Share your letter with a partner.

The Gigantic REDWOODS

A Memoir by Mrs. J. B. Rideout

retold by M. J. Cosson

I'll never forget the summer of 1888. I was invited by friends to join them on a camping trip in northern California. We rode in a covered wagon and slept in tents.

Early in our travels, we decided to see the gigantic redwoods. About two miles on our journey we began to wind our way upward around the side of a high mountain. The weather was hot. After the first few miles, the mountain was so steep that the children walked. The miles seemed to lengthen out until we felt that we had come twenty at least. Around a turn in the road, we were relieved to find a large trough filled with water from a cold spring.

What was unforgettable about the summer of 1888?

After we ate a good lunch, we started on. In a short time we were among the gigantic redwoods. Words cannot express the beauty of these grand old kings of the forest. They are large and tall and straight, narrowing gradually to the faraway tops. We were all quite excited. We raced to look out first on one side of the wagon and then on the other. Every few minutes the boys would jump out and measure a tree, until they found one that was more than forty feet around!

It was now cool and pleasant. We soon began to go down, down the mountain. We could see the road winding back and forth below us. There were places that made me feel dizzy to look down.

It was nearly sundown when we reached the bottom of the hill at a place called Low Gap. We were allowed to camp near the spring. The boys were told that they could not hunt the quail in the wood. The quail were so tame that they came up to eat with the chickens we had with us.

> How would you describe the trip so far?

Low Gap was a very gloomy place. Its surroundings were tall, thick woods. As darkness settled around us, we girls became somewhat afraid. We talked of grizzly bears, mountain lions, and other beasts of prey.

Read, Cover, Remember, Retell Technique With a partner, take turns reading as much text as you can cover with your hand. Then cover up what you read and retell the information to your partner.

We had a lively time in the morning, however. Our recreation was shooing away pigs that smelled our breakfast. The pigs were determined to share it with us! We were glad when we were ready to continue our upward way.

We came to a good camping place as the sun was sinking among the distant trees. The low sun pierced our surroundings with its flying arrows of gold. The boys pitched the tents.

We gazed in wonder and admiration upon untouched nature. We looked down upon the trees in the canyon. They were hundreds of feet below us, in the shadow of the distant rising cliffs. From where we stood, the tops of the trees seemed all on a level.

Beyond the canyon, the massive redwoods were visible from the roots to the branches. What an army of monsters! They nodded their lofty heads to the ocean wind that marched along the high land. They seemed to be a troop of giant soldiers climbing the mountain.

What did the redwoods look like from the campsite?

The next morning, we wound our way slowly along the mountain. We were startled to see, directly below us, the great feathery top of one of the giant trees falling slowly through the air. The axe had done its work.

The cone of bright green slowly disappeared beneath the waving leaves. It reminded me of a vessel that disappears beneath the sea. But oh, the crash that followed! We could feel the mountain tremble as the thunder of the fall arose from the dark canyon below. It echoed among the surrounding mountains.

Do you think many of the men who lived in the area worked as loggers? Why might this be true?

Our driver started up the horses, and our wagon again moved along the winding road. We soon reached the place where they had been cutting down the redwoods. The trees had been cut off several feet above the ground. We wondered why it was done and how. As there was a man near making railroad ties, we asked him about it.

He said the timber near the roots was not easy to work, and it was a hard job to saw a log off. First they cut through the bark, then drove in wedges, then built a platform to stand on. Finally, they cut the tree off as high up as they thought best.

Near the road where we stopped stood one of the largest barns we had seen. The owner said it was large enough for four horses, wagons, and eight bales of hay. This barn was a huge hollow stump with a door in one side! Fire had burned it out, leaving only a shell. The gentleman laughed at our astonishment. He told us that a few miles over in the woods a large family was living in a stump!

Why were people able to use the redwood stumps for barns and houses?

Dear Eda,

I was just thinking about our camping trip and had to write you. I can still see that stack of cut logs. They were immense. Do you remember how someone had written on the ends of some of them, "This is a buster," "This is the boss," "Hard to beat?" They surely were hard to beat!

Your Friend,

Linnie

Think and Respond

Reflect and Write

- You and your partner took turns reading and retelling sections of the memoir, *The Gigantic Redwoods*.

- Choose one of the sections you read. On one side of an index card, write what you know from reading the text. On the back of the card, write what new information you now understand.

Homonyms in Context

Reread *The Gigantic Redwoods: A Memoir* by Mrs. J. B. Rideout to find examples of homonyms. Then select three of the words you found to use in sentences. Share your favorite sentence with a partner.

Turn and Talk

SYNTHESIZE

Discuss with a partner what have you learned so far about what it means to synthesize?

- How do you synthesize information as you read?

- How can synthesizing make you a better reader?

Choose one of the ideas you synthesized for a section of *The Gigantic Redwoods: A Memoir* by Mrs. J. B. Rideout. Compare your work with that of a partner. Are your new ideas similar? If not, how do they differ?

Critical Thinking

With a partner talk about how landforms, such as mountains and deserts, affect the lives of people. Skim *The Gigantic Redwoods* and make a list of the landforms mentioned. For each landform, write one word reflecting how people may be affected by that landform or the reaction that Mrs. Rideout has to that landform. Answer these questions.

- Based on *The Gigantic Redwoods*, what do you think are the main landforms of northern California?

- How did people adapt to life in this region?

- How does this story support the theme that land shapes people's lives?

Come to the Oregon Coast

Are you looking for a vacation place with beautiful **surroundings**? Then come to the coast of Oregon!

The coast stretches for almost 300 miles along the Pacific Ocean. You'll see ocean views, beaches,

rugged cliffs, and forests. And you'll find endless opportunities for **recreation**. You can fish, windsurf, or even go whale watching. Or maybe you just want to relax. How about taking long walks on the beach?

Maybe you enjoy vacationing at a higher **altitude**. We have something for you, too. The coastal mountains are just a short drive away. They rise to a height of more than 4,000 feet.

The coast is dotted with **port** after port. Inland is the lovely city of Portland. The ports and the city offer interesting shops and fine restaurants.

Whatever you want in a vacation spot, you'll have easy **access** to it in coastal Oregon. We'll be looking for you!

Structured Vocabulary Discussion

Work with a partner or in a small group to think of vocabulary words that would fill in the following blanks. Be sure you can explain how the words are related.

Study is to *school* as _____ is *vacation*.

Depth is to *oceans* as _____ is to *mountains*.

> Throughout the week, add to your vocabulary journal entries. Record new insights and other words that relate to this week's vocabulary.

Picture It

Copy this word organizer into your vocabulary journal. Fill in the empty circles with examples of different types of **surroundings.**

forests

surroundings

Copy this word organizer into your vocabulary journal. Fill in the blanks with some things you might find in a **port.**

port
boats

KEY WEST
Florida

by Sue Miller

Key West is an island—a very small island. It is only about 4 miles long and 1.5 miles wide!

Key West is the southernmost U.S. city in North America. The Florida Keys is a chain of islands about 100 miles from the Florida mainland.

Until the 1900s, people had to take a boat to reach the island. A state highway, built in 1938, connects the mainland with the island. The highway includes one bridge that is seven miles long!

Life on the island has not always been easy. Fire destroyed the city in 1859. Hurricanes have also struck Key West many times.

In the past, people in Key West made their living fishing. Today, tourism is the island's main industry. Deep-sea fishing and sightseeing boats dock at Key West's port. Key West hosts many boat races.

The style of old Key West houses is well-suited to the climate. The light-colored roofs reflect the hot Florida sun. And the shuttered windows protect the houses from hurricane winds.

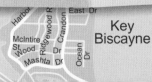

Snowboarding IN VERMONT

Have you ever wanted to snowboard? Thousands of people, young and old, enjoy the sport. Many people in Vermont have helped publicize the sport.

Jake Burton Carpenter is one of the sport's pioneers. He started a snowboarding company in Vermont in 1977. He has worked hard to extend the sport's popularity.

The task hasn't always been easy. Early snowboarders had to conquer the concerns of skiers. Skiers argued that snowboarders took too many risks and damaged the snow with their boards. Many ski resorts worried that snowboarders would get in the way of skiers and even cause injuries. Eventually, the resorts banned snowboarding.

Vermont was the first state to open its slopes to snowboarders. Today, most ski resorts maintain slopes for snowboarding. Snowboarders compete in the Winter Olympics. Maybe one day, you'll join them!

Verbs

Activity One

About Verbs

Some verbs are action words, such as *run*, *talk*, and *jump*. In sentences, verbs explain the action of the subject. As your teacher reads *Snowboarding in Vermont* listen for the verbs.

Verbs in Context

With a partner, read *Snowboarding in Vermont* and look for the verbs. Make a chart like the one below. List all of the verbs you find and their meanings.

VERB	MEANING
publicize	make known

Activity Two

Explore Words Together

Work with a partner to a write a sentence with an action verb for each person or object in the list on the right. Here is an example: The airplane *landed* on the runway.

doctor	computer
airplane	soldier
student	tree

Activity Three

Explore Words in Writing

Write an interesting paragraph from a book you like. Now study the text and find the verbs. Then think of other verbs that would work just as well in the sentences. Rewrite the passage using your verbs. Share your paragraph with a partner.

MOUNTAIN HOMESTEAD

by Linda Lott

"**W**e're going to lose our Bertie, our firstborn child," Mother said in a shaky voice as she watched the doctor leave.

"Don't give up hope yet," Father replied. "Not everyone who gets diphtheria dies."

"No," Mother answered bitterly. "But Doc says the germ stays in the damp soil here in rainy old Seattle. What if there's another really bad outbreak, like 1875?"

"That was 35 years ago," Father said.

"Still," Mother replied, "Henry could get sick. We could lose our son. Doc says we would all be healthier in a higher, drier place."

Father pulled out a pamphlet. "Would you really be willing to move? The government has opened land for homesteading in the forests around Coville. The land is high and dry, and it's there for the taking. All we need to do is build a homestead and work it for five years. The government will even give us seeds to plant."

What is homesteading?

"Could we possibly manage a homestead?" Mother wondered.

"We're strong and determined, and we both grew up on farms," said Father. "We can do anything we set our minds to!"

That was how the adventure began. Father rushed off to file a claim. Within a few weeks Mother and Father had sold everything but the essentials they would need on the homestead. As soon as Bertie was healthy enough to travel, Mother, Father, Bertie, and Henry set off for their new home.

The homestead was high on a mountain. At that altitude the air was fresh, and the view was spectacular. Everywhere the family looked, they saw lush, green trees.

The family got right to work. Father and Henry cleared enough land for the cabin. It was hard work. They cut down the trees and struggled to dig up the stumps. The cabin they built wasn't fancy. It had one large main room and a sleeping loft for Bertie and Henry. Mother and Father slept in a lean-to that was attached to the main house.

What clues help you to understand the meaning of the word *spectacular*?

Reverse Think-Aloud Technique Listen as your partner reads part of the text aloud. Choose a point in the text to stop your partner and ask what he or she is thinking about the text at that moment. Then switch roles with your partner.

Slowly Father and Henry cleared more land. Father sold the logs to the local mill. Farming proved to be more difficult than Father had expected, though. The family worked long, hard days. They were able to grow enough crops for their own use, but there was never anything left over to sell.

What strategy helps you figure out the meaning of the word *eventually*?

One evening, the family gathered outside the door to watch the sunset. "We've done well," Father said. "We have a roof over our head and enough food to eat. But we'll eventually run out of trees to cut and sell."

Father had a plan. He could earn money working at the logging mill. "I'll only be able to come home on weekends," he said. "Bertie and Henry, you will have to help your mother take care of the farm."

Bertie and Henry exchanged glances. Father's job would mean another big change and more hard work. But both children bravely responded, "We can do it!"

RIVERSIDE AVENUE, A BUSY STREET IN PROGRESSIVE SPOKANE. "ON UNION PACIFIC SYSTEM."

Over the years, the family settled into a pleasant life. The children's days were filled with chores and school. The highlight of every week was the day Father returned from the logging mill. He sometimes brought surprises, and he always brought money. Mother kept the money in a safe place near the fireplace.

One evening Father came home with a huge grin on his face. "Fetch the money jar," he shouted. The children watched as Father carefully counted the money. Then he revealed his big surprise.

How are the words *revealed* and *surprise* related?

"We've been here for more than five years," he said. "I don't want the children to forget what a city is like, so we're off to Spokane for a little vacation." Everyone gave a cheer.

Early the next morning, Mother, Father, Bertie, and Henry dressed in their best clothes and boarded the train for the long trip to Spokane. Their first stop in the city was a restaurant where the children could order whatever they wanted.

That night the family stayed in a hotel for the first time in their lives. They could hardly sleep, though, because the next day, they were going to ride a roller coaster in the park.

What a wonderful time they had in the city! As they waited to board the train to go home, Father looked thoughtful.

"We all enjoyed the city," he said. "Maybe it's time to consider moving back."

"The city is exciting," said Mother. "I'd miss our quiet life in the mountains, though."

"I'd love to have access to a roller coaster every day," said Henry, "but I'd miss my friends from home."

"I'm not sick anymore," said Bertie. "I could live in the city, but I'm happiest outdoors in the fresh mountain air."

Imagine that you are a character in this story. Which life would you choose?

"I guess it's settled then," said Father as they boarded the train. "We're not city people any longer. The homestead is our true home."

Think and Respond

Reflect and Write

- You and your partner took turns reading *Mountain Homestead*. Discuss the questions you asked and your answers.

- On one side of an index card, write the words or ideas you found difficult. On the other side of the index card, write the fix-up strategy you used to figure out the meanings.

Verbs in Context

Reread *Mountain Homestead* to find examples of verbs. Write down at least five verbs you find. Compare your list with a partner. Then work together to write a paragraph using the verbs.

Turn and Talk

FIX-UP STRATEGIES

Discuss with a partner hat have you learned so far about fix-up strategies.

- What are some strategies to use when you are having difficulty understanding a passage or text?

Choose one problem you had while reading *Mountain Homestead*. Explain to a partner how you used a fix-up strategy to solve the problem.

Critical Thinking

With a partner, talk about what your lives might be like if you built a homestead in a mountain wilderness area. List the supplies you think you would need and the activities you might need to do. Look back through *Mountain Homestead*. Write down the supplies the family used and the activities that they participated in. Then discuss these questions with a partner:

- What were the landforms around the homestead?

- What advantages and disadvantages did these landforms present for the family?

- How does this story support the theme that the land shapes people's lives?

Maridalen, 1852
Johann Christial Clausen Dahl (1788–1857)

THEME 7   **Why Does Water Move?**

THEME 8   **What Makes Soil Different?**

Viewing

The artist who painted this picture was famous for painting landscapes of his native country, Norway. Maridalen, a small town in Norway, is barely visible in the center background of the painting.

1. Study the painting. What does the movement of the water appear to be doing to the land?

2. How does the artist create water movement in the painting?

3. What can you learn about the relationship between soil and water from the painting?

In This UNIT

In this unit, you will read about why waves move and how soil is formed. You will also learn about different types of soil.

Why Does Water Move?

Contents

Modeled Reading

Realistic Fiction Very Last First Time
by Jan Andrews 192

Vocabulary
visible, tide, shore, chisel, wedge 194

Comprehension Strategy ✎
Monitor Understanding 196

Shared Reading

Procedural **Making Waves** by Katie Sharp 198

Grammar
Helping Verbs 200

Interactive Reading

Adventure Typhoon! by John Manos 202

Vocabulary
swift, analyze, model, current, coastline 208

Poem "The Vessel" by M. J. Cosson 210

Word Study
Inflected Endings -ed, -ing, and -s 212

Persuasive Essay Fighting Coastal Erosion:
Why We Should Save Our Coastal Wetlands
by Mary Dylewski 214

Genre
Realistic Fiction

Very Last First Time

BY JAN ANDREWS   ILLUSTRATED BY IAN WALLACE

Precise Listening

Precise listening is listening to understand characters. Listen to the focus questions your teacher will read to you.

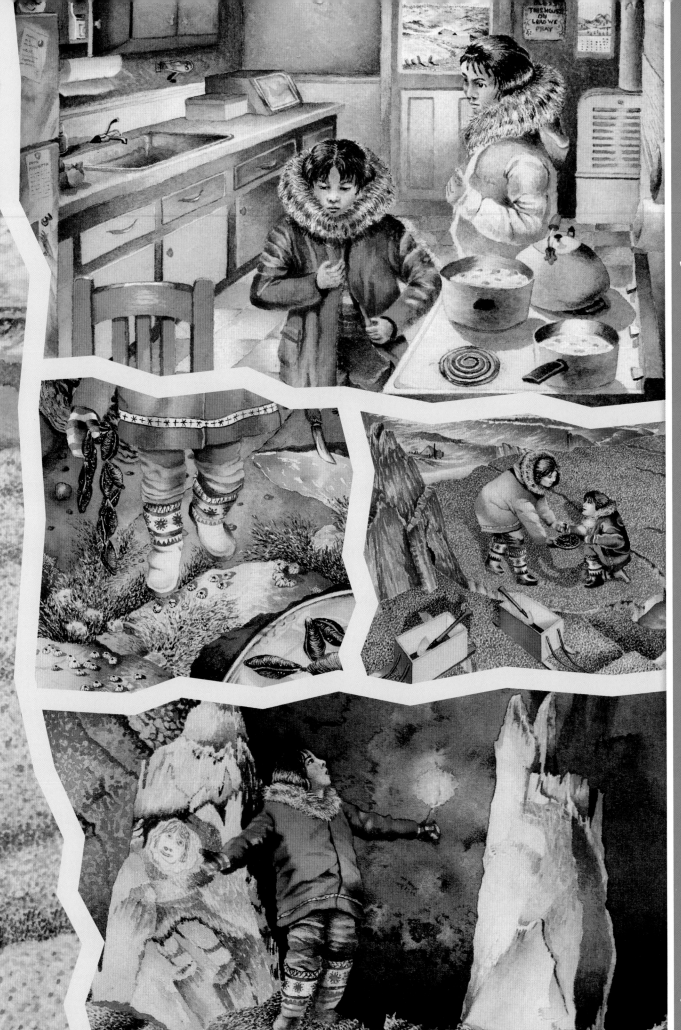

LEARNING ABOUT THE INUIT

October 28

Dear Jim,

Well, I've been in Canada for over a month now. This student exchange program is great. I'm staying with an Inuit family. Their last name is Ulujuk. The Ulujuks live in a village on the **shore** of Pelly Bay, a small area of the Arctic Ocean shaped like a **wedge**.

The village is in Nunavut, the Inuit province in Canada. Nunavut is so far north that the North Pole is **visible**. I'm just kidding—but it is really far north. We're actually inside the Arctic Circle!

It's also really, really COLD. Pretty soon we'll need a **chisel** to break the ice off things.

The Ulujuk family has a son named Arwela. He's teaching me some Inuit words. Today when the **tide** was coming in, he splashed his hand through a wave and said, "imek." That's the Inuit word for water.

I'll be home at the start of winter break. I'll see you then.

Steve

Structured Vocabulary Discussion

When your teacher says a vocabulary word, have the people in your group take turns saying the first word they think of. Continue until your teacher says, "Stop." Then have the last person who said a word explain how his or her word is related to the vocabulary word.

Throughout the week, add to your vocabulary journal entries. Record new insights and other words that relate to this week's vocabulary.

Picture It

Copy this word organizer into your vocabulary journal. Fill in the blanks with a few things that are clearly **visible** only with a microscope.

visible

grain of sand

Copy this word organizer into your vocabulary journal. Fill in the sections with things that can resemble a **wedge**.

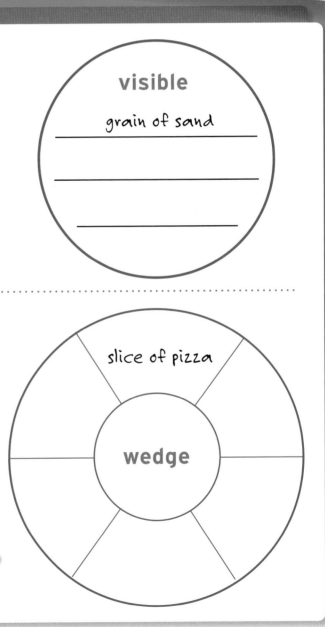

slice of pizza

wedge

Monitor Understanding

As you read, take time to monitor understanding. Every so often stop and think about what you have read. See if you understand what you have read so far. This will help you determine if there are any parts you do not understand.

Check to make sure you are UNDERSTANDING what you read.

Strategies

Check your understanding. When you don't understand, try a few key strategies to help.

TURN AND TALK Listen to your teacher read the following lines from *Very Last First Time*. Discuss with a partner what has already happened by answering the following questions.

• What is the passage about?

• What do the sounds Eva hears indicate?

Beyond the rock pool, seaweed was piled in thick, shiny heaps and masses. Eva scrambled over the seaweed, up and onto a rock mound. Stretching her arms wide, tilting her head back, she laughed, imagining the shifting, waving, lifting swirl of seaweed when the tide comes in.

The tide!

Eva listened. The lap, lap of the waves sounded louder and nearer. Whoosh and roar and whoosh again.

TAKE IT WITH YOU Retelling what you have read is a good way to monitor understanding. If you cannot retell what has already happened, reread the parts of the text that are unclear. As you read other selections, use a chart like the one below to help you monitor understanding.

Page Where I Noticed I Didn't Understand	What I Did						Which One Worked?
	Reread	Reflected On Purpose	Thought About Meaning	Asked Myself Questions	Thought About Strategies	Used Genre Knowledge	
The page where Eva is walking on the ocean floor to collect mussels. She heard the sound of the waves getting louder and nearer.	✔	✔	✔	✔	✔	✔	I reread the information about the tide. This helped me understand what the sounds indicate.

Making Waves

by Katie Sharp

If you want to study waves, you might go to an ocean or lake. There you could watch waves crashing on the shore. But what if the nearest ocean or lake were hundreds of miles away? Is there a way you can bring waves to your classroom?

The best way to study waves in your classroom is to make a model. A model is a copy of something that can be found in the real world. Models are a good way to study things that would be difficult or impossible to study firsthand.

Making a Wave Model With a few supplies, you can study waves right at your desk.

What You Will Need

- a plastic soda bottle with lid
- blue food coloring
- mineral or baby oil

What You Will Do Look at the flow chart on the next page. It shows how to make two different kinds of wave models. Follow the directions in the flow chart to determine which model best illustrates the movement of waves.

Note: You may need an adult to help you with some of the steps.

Activity Follow-up What are some other models that you could use to study something that may be otherwise too difficult to study in person?

How to Choose the Best Wave Model

Water Only Model

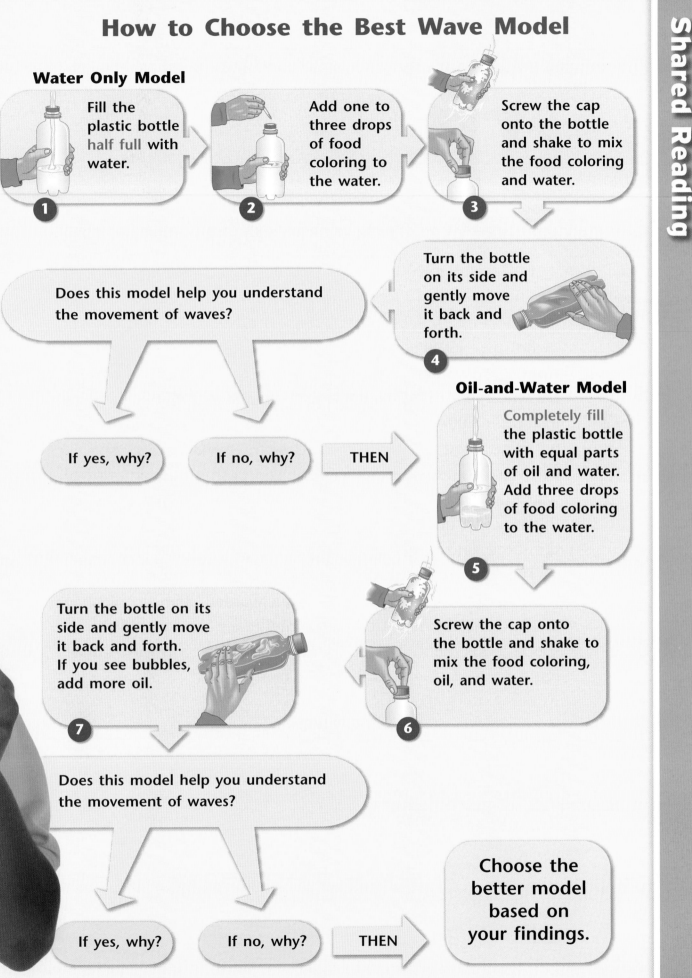

1 Fill the plastic bottle half full with water.

2 Add one to three drops of food coloring to the water.

3 Screw the cap onto the bottle and shake to mix the food coloring and water.

4 Turn the bottle on its side and gently move it back and forth.

Does this model help you understand the movement of waves?

If yes, why?

If no, why?

THEN

Oil-and-Water Model

5 Completely fill the plastic bottle with equal parts of oil and water. Add three drops of food coloring to the water.

6 Screw the cap onto the bottle and shake to mix the food coloring, oil, and water.

7 Turn the bottle on its side and gently move it back and forth. If you see bubbles, add more oil.

Does this model help you understand the movement of waves?

If yes, why?

If no, why?

THEN

Choose the better model based on your findings.

Epicenter

Shockwaves

Tsunami!

In December 2004, a huge ocean wave smashed into lands around the Indian Ocean. This type of wave is called a tsunami (soo-NAH-mee). A tsunami travels as a low wave that moves as fast as a jet airliner. When the wave gets close to land, the water has to slow down. This causes the wave to pile up. It becomes very tall. When the wave hits shore, water washes far inland. In 2004, many lives were lost when the wave rushed in.

These huge waves are created in three main ways. An earthquake under the ocean floor can push a vast amount of water up, creating a wave. The 2004 wave was produced in this way. An underwater landslide or volcano can also cause the same kind of gigantic wave.

The 2004 wave caught people by surprise. There was no warning system. If people had been warned, some could have escaped the danger. Area governments are now putting in special equipment. This equipment can sense a wave. People hope this will save lives in future tsunamis.

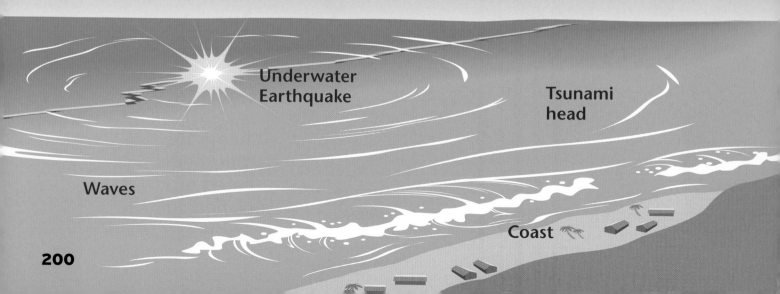

Underwater Earthquake

Tsunami head

Waves

Coast

Helping Verbs

Activity One

About Helping Verbs

A helping verb works with the main verb in a sentence to tell about an action. The helping verb always comes before the main verb. *Am, is, are, was, were, has, have, had, will, would, can,* and *could* are examples of helping verbs. Listen for the helping verbs as your teacher reads about tsunamis.

Helping Verbs in Context

With a partner, reread the information about tsunamis and find the helping verbs. Make a chart like the one below. Write the helping verb in the first column. In the second column, write a short sentence using the verb.

WORD	SENTENCE
is	My sister is going to the park.

Activity Two

Explore Words Together

The list on the right contains helping verbs. Work with a partner to write a paragraph in which every sentence contains a helping verb and a main verb. Now see if you can rewrite the paragraph without any helping verbs. You may find that it's almost impossible to express the same thoughts without the helping verbs.

is	were
are	has
was	had

Activity Three

Explore Words in Writing

Pick a page from a book you enjoy reading. See how many helping verbs the author uses on the page. Then rewrite three of the author's sentences using different helping verbs. Share your sentences with a partner.

Typhoon!

by John Manos

Marguerite couldn't believe her eyes as she stared through the side windows of the ship's pilothouse. Rushing toward them was a wave that was taller than an eight-story building! She shouted, "Roberto! Help!"

Describe what astonished Marguerite about the wave she saw.

Her 14-year-old brother spun around, his mouth falling open. Then he leaped to Marguerite's side. They fought with the wheel to turn the ship toward the monstrous wave. Its movement was so swift that it seemed they could not possibly save the ship!

How can this be? Marguerite thought. *Our trip began so nicely!*

* * *

Just three days earlier, Marguerite and Roberto had flown to meet their Aunt Pilar in Australia. The next day they were on a ship in the Coral Sea.

For Marguerite, nothing could have been better than sailing on an expedition to study animals. Even though she was just nine, Marguerite had already decided she wanted to work as a biologist, like Aunt Pilar.

Aunt Pilar was studying box jellyfish. "Box jellyfish?" Roberto had asked. "What an odd name!"

"It's just a description," Aunt Pilar had said. She had shown them one that swam in a tank. It was almost a cube!

"How funny-looking!" Marguerite had laughed. But when she started to reach into the water, Aunt Pilar had almost shrieked.

"Don't!" she had cried. "Box jellyfish have a terribly painful sting," she had explained. "Some are even deadly!"

> Why does Marguerite think the box jellyfish is strange?

Aunt Pilar had told them that box jellyfish do not drift in the water like other jellyfish. They swim around, chasing food. They have 24 eyes. What's more, she had said, they have four brains!

"Stop!" Roberto had blurted. "They sound like they come from outer space!"

Just then, Captain Li had walked in to warn everyone to prepare for an approaching typhoon.

"What's a typhoon?" Roberto had asked.

"They're called hurricanes in America," Captain Li had answered. "But typhoons spin in the opposite direction from hurricanes."

Read, Cover, Remember, Retell Technique With a partner, take turns reading as much text as you can cover with your hand. Then cover up what you read and retell the information to your partner.

"Can't we just sail back to port to escape the typhoon?" Marguerite had wondered.

"We're actually safer in deep water," Captain Li had replied. "If the sea gets very rough, we just have to point the ship's bow—the front—into the waves. That way, the ship will ride up one side of the wave and down the other. Picture how a toy boat acts on a lake when the water gets rough. That's a good model for what happens in a typhoon."

"What happens if we don't face the ship into a big wave?" Roberto had asked.

Captain Li explained the danger. "If a large wave strikes the ship from the side, it could make the ship capsize, or roll over. A wave that strikes the ship from the rear could drive the bow beneath the waves and force the ship under."

"Don't frighten the children, Captain Li," Pilar had said, looking quite worried.

"I'm sorry," Captain Li had said. "Don't worry, children. I have experience with typhoons; we'll be fine."

What does Captain Li explain to Marguerite?

But as the day went on, the sky had clouded over and the sea had become rougher and rougher. The wind had gotten fiercer by the hour. "I'm getting nervous," Roberto had said. "What's worse is, Captain Li seems to be getting nervous, too."

It was true, the captain had stopped smiling and laughing. He moved quickly from place to place on the ship and constantly checked the wind and measured wave heights. Finally, Roberto had asked why.

"Wind is what causes big waves," Captain Li had explained.

Roberto and Marguerite had exchanged a scared look.

Captain Li had smiled to reassure them. "We'll be fine as long as we don't get hit by a rogue wave. That's when one of these waves meets another wave. If the timing is just right, then a much larger wave could hit us, and it might come from a different direction."

What is Captain Li most worried about?

Just then, Captain Li had been called away—the storm had broken one of the fuel lines. Captain Li had set the ship's wheel and rushed off to remedy the problem.

About fifteen minutes later, Marguerite had looked through the window and had seen a wave that was larger than anything she could imagine. It was sweeping down on the ship—and it would hit them broadside! That was when she screamed.

* * *

Now, she and Roberto struggled with the ship's wheel. They desperately tried to turn the bow toward the monster wave. The ship was changing direction, but only very slowly—too slowly! They both pulled on the wheel with all their strength. In the rolling water, the rudder fought them.

The wave seemed to fill the sky. It was at least 90 feet high. "Pull!" Marguerite shouted.

They heard the pilothouse door fly open and suddenly strong hands joined theirs on the wheel. Captain Li grunted as he fought to turn the ship. As the huge wave blocked the sight of everything else through the pilothouse windows, he finally turned the bow to face it.

The ship crawled up the face of the wave—up and up, higher and higher! Finally, the bow broke through the crest. Marguerite and Roberto fell to the floor of the pilothouse as the ship slid down the back of the wave.

Then they heard the strangest sound of all: clapping. Two crew members were applauding them! "Well done!" said Captain Li. Marguerite was sure that she saw the box jellyfish wink one of its 24 eyes.

Describe why the crew clapped for Marguerite and Roberto.

Think and Respond

Reflect and Write

- You and your partner took turns retelling sections of *Typhoon!* Choose one of the sections you read and recall what action you took to help your understanding.

- On one side of an index card, describe the part of the text you had trouble understanding. On the back of the card tell what you did to make the meaning clear.

Helping Verbs in Context

Reread *Typhoon!* to find examples of helping verbs. Write down the words you find. Then write a paragraph using as many of the words as you can. Share your paragraph with a partner.

Turn and Talk

MONITOR UNDERSTANDING

Discuss with a partner what you have learned so far about how to monitor understanding while you read.

- What does it mean to monitor understanding?

- How do you monitor understanding?

Reread *Typhoon!* Then reread the description you and a partner created for the Reflect and Write activity. Discuss whether any of the retellings need revision and why. Revise the descriptions, if needed.

Critical Thinking

With a partner, brainstorm what you know about wind, waves, and typhoons. Write your ideas on a sheet of paper. Look back at *Typhoon!* and find the information presented by Captain Li about rogue waves. With your partner, write a description of how a rogue wave could put a ship in danger. Then answer these questions.

- How does a typhoon affect waves?

- How could a ship protect itself from being turned over or sunk by a large wave?

On a Mississippi Riverboat

August 23, 1860, 9 P.M.

I'm so glad Father let me come along on this trip to New Orleans. I'm looking forward to seeing the Louisiana **coastline**.

Father is a wonderful riverboat pilot. It's really amazing how he can **analyze** the river. Even at night, he always sees the signs of underwater rocks and **swift** waters.

Today, he impressed all the passengers with his skills. A sandbar blocked our way. Sandbars form where the **current** is weak. They're a real problem in late summer, when the river is low. Father let the boat drift right up to the sandbar with the engines off. Then he ordered them turned up to full. The two paddlewheels on the sides of the boat walked us right over the bar to the next stretch of water.

I received a great present on the trip. A crew member made a **model** of a steamboat for me. The paddlewheels even work. I'll keep it forever.

Structured Vocabulary Discussion

Work with a partner to complete the following sentences about your vocabulary words.

Read is to *analyze* as *shore* is to _____.

Gusty is to *wind* as *swift* is to _____.

> Throughout the week, add to your vocabulary journal entries. Record new insights and other words that relate to this week's vocabulary.

Picture It

Copy this word organizer into your vocabulary journal. Fill in the sections with things people like to **analyze**.

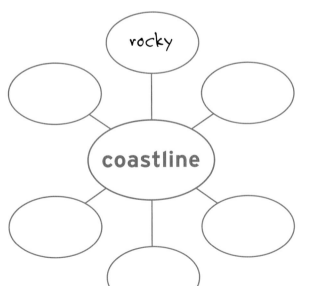

analyze	
puzzles	

Copy this word organizer into your vocabulary journal. Fill in the circles with words that can describe a **coastline**.

rocky

coastline

The Vessel

by M. J. Cosson

A secret someone sends a message in a vessel.

The vessel, a bottle, bobs on the waves,

Like a dizzy kid on a carnival ride,

Circling from cliff to cape to bay,

Night upon day, flowing and floating and
following the flotsam

On an uncharted trip round and round.

Now gaining bearings and following a course,

Straight as an arrow or as the gull flies,

Like a messenger on a mission, a pirate stalking prey,

A clipper ship carrying precious goods across the sea,

The vessel shoots with the current toward a land far away.

Like a bold surfer, it catches tall ridges,
Bumping and bouncing to untold heights,
Tossing and tumbling with laughing delight,
Joyously joining the curve of the wave,
And sliding the sea with slick, silly senselessness.

The winking moon man looks down from the sky,
Says, "Enough play, move on," and nudges it along.
Crabs, clams, weeds, seeds, and shells from below
Wash with it, under a star blinky sky, onto the
     powdery-soft shimmery shore.
The vessel waits to be plucked up, opened like a shell,
     its insides digested.

Water and Gravity

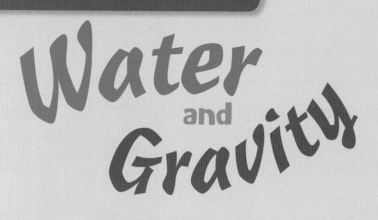

Moon

Lunar Gravity

Earth

Ocean Level

Gravity Rules!

Ocean tides are caused by the Moon's gravity dragging ocean water slightly toward the Moon. The Sun's gravity also plays a part in tides.

low tide

high tide

Oceans are shaped into a huge bulge with sloping sides by the Moon's gravity. The sides slope very gradually, but the bulge covers a vast area. Billions of tons of seawater slowly move toward the Moon's pull. When a coastal area is near the center of the bulge, it has high tide. When it is at the side of the bulge, the water level has dropped. The area then has low tide.

Fun Fact! Earth's gravity plays a role in ocean currents. Cold water is heavier than warm water. Gravity pulls cold water down. As it sinks to the bottom, the cold water forces other water away, creating currents.

Did You Know? Gravity influences the Earth and everything on it. When you jump, gravity causes you to be pulled back to the ground. Without gravity, you would find yourself drifting off into space.

Inflected Endings
-ed, -ing, and -s

Activity One

About Inflected Endings

An inflected ending is an addition to the end of a word that changes the word's form in some way. For example, -ed added to *pull* results in *pulled*. The -ed added to the root word is the inflected ending. As your teacher reads the information about water and gravity, listen for words with inflected endings.

Inflected Endings in Context

Reread *Water and Gravity* and make a list of all the words with inflected endings. Write down each word, its meaning, and the root word. Note that with some words, adding an inflected ending requires doubling the final letter of the root word.

WORD	MEANING	ROOT
dropped	fallen	drop

Activity Two

Explore Words Together

With a partner, think of as many words as you can that can be made into new words with all of the endings -ed, -ing, and -s. Use the words listed at the right to get started.

mail	spill
rake	hope
hop	plan

Activity Three

Explore Words in Writing

Write a paragraph about any subject that interests you, using as many words with inflected endings as you can think of. Share your paragraph with a partner.

FIGHTING
Coastal Erosion

Why We Should Save Our Coastal Wetlands

by Mary Dylewski

Swamps and marshes are types of coastal wetlands. Some wetlands are covered by water. Others have very wet soil. Wetlands serve many purposes. The plants and soils in wetlands filter the water that runs off the land. This process helps keep oceans clean. Wetlands are important habitats for wildlife.

Those are all good reasons for protecting wetlands. There is another good reason. Wetlands help prevent coastal erosion.

Why are coastal wetlands important?

What Is Coastal Erosion?

Erosion is any process that moves bits of rocks and soil from place to place. Water, wind, and gravity cause erosion. Living things do, too. Oceans are the main force in coastal erosion. Waves, currents, and tides wear away the rocks and soil. Some of this material washes out to sea.

Erosion is eating away the U.S. coastline at an alarming rate. The coasts along the Gulf of Mexico and the Atlantic Ocean are the hardest hit. The Atlantic coast loses about 2 to 3 feet each year. On an average, the Gulf coast loses six feet or more each year! Some areas lose much more. As Hurricane Katrina showed in 2005, a major hurricane can increase erosion very quickly.

What causes coastal erosion?

Sand carried away by current

Wave Action

Bank

Coast

Bank

Coast

Partner Jigsaw Technique Read a section of the essay with a partner and write down one main idea or important detail. Be prepared to summarize your section and share one new idea you synthesized.

How Serious Is the Problem?

Six feet a year might not sound like much. But those feet add up! Scientists warn that houses and other structures built within 500 feet of the water's edge are in danger in high erosion areas. Major storms add to the danger. A powerful hurricane can wipe out 100 or more feet of coast in a single day!

The Gulf coast is home to more than half of the nation's wetlands. However, these wetlands are eroding at a rapid rate. Louisiana loses about one football field of wetlands every 20 minutes! The state is also losing its small coastal islands, which protect the mainland from the open sea. Katrina sped the process of loss. Only time will tell how much of this land will recover.

Which area of the country has the most coastal wetlands?

Location of Coastal Wetlands in the U.S.
(excluding Hawaii and Alaska)

Pacific Coast 2%

Atlantic Coast 47%

Gulf Coast 51%

216

How Can Saving the Wetlands Help?

Healthy wetlands slow erosion. They do this in several ways that we can measure and analyze. Wetlands protect the coast from the forces of normal waves and currents. Because they are between the water and the land, coastal wetlands lessen the force with which waves and currents strike the coast.

Coastal wetlands can also reduce the impact of a storm surge. A storm surge is a very large wave that is pushed toward the coast by strong winds.

Coastal wetlands also trap loose soil, rock, and sand that are carried by water. The roots of wetland plants trap these materials and hold them in place. This trapping helps prevent further erosion.

Mississippi

Louisiana

How do coastal wetlands help stop erosion?

Why Do We Need to Take Action?

People are beginning to understand the importance of coastal wetlands. The national government has passed laws to protect these areas. So have several state governments. Many citizens groups are also working to protect the wetlands.

We can protect and even rebuild the wetlands. The task won't be easy, however. And it won't be cheap. However, lost property, lost jobs, and lost lives are the prices for doing nothing. I think it is too high a price. I urge you to support restoring our coastal wetlands. We can't afford to keep losing our coastline.

How are national and state governments working to protect the coastal wetlands?

Think and Respond

Reflect and Write

- You and your partner have read sections of *Fighting Coastal Erosion: Why We Should Save Our Coastal Wetlands*. Discuss the details of the section you read and the new idea you formed.

- On one side of an index card, write the new idea you synthesized. On the other side of the index card, write two or more details that helped you synthesize this idea. Find partner teams that read other sections. Share summaries and new ideas.

Inflected Endings in Context

Reread *Fighting Coastal Erosion: Why We Should Save Our Coastal Wetlands* to find examples of words with the inflected endings -*ed*, -*ing*, and -*s*. Work with a partner to see who can find the most words. Then each of you use some of the words to write three sentences that argue for or against protecting coastal wetlands. Share your favorite sentence with your partner.

Turn and Talk

SYNTHESIZE

Discuss with a partner what you have learned so far about how to synthesize what you read.

- What is synthesizing? How do you bring details together to create a new idea?

Choose one of the syntheses you created for a section of *Fighting Coastal Erosion: Why We Should Save Our Coastal Wetlands*. Compare your synthesis with that of a partner. How are your and your partner's syntheses alike? How are they different?

Critical Thinking

In a small group, talk about coastal wetlands. Write a description of coastal wetlands by listing their characteristics. Look back at *Fighting Coastal Erosion*. Compare the description your group created with the description of coastal wetlands in the selection. Then discuss these questions.

- How do waves, currents, and tides contribute to coastal erosion?

- How do wetlands help slow the effects of erosion?

- Why is it important to protect coastal wetlands? Explain your answer.

Contents

Modeled Reading

Expository The Living Earth by Eleonore Schmid...............222

Vocabulary
consist, geology, property, layer, artificial...........................224

Comprehension Strategy
Ask Questions...226

Shared Reading

Fantasy A Very Dirty Subject by Karen Lowther.................228

Grammar
Adjectives..230

Interactive Reading

Personal Narrative The Case of Vanishing Soil
by Darlene Stille...232

Vocabulary
combine, separate, texture, replace, particles......................238

Poem "What Does Weather Do to Soil?"
by Ann Weil...240

Word Study
Prefix *un-*..242

Realistic Fiction The Black Blizzard
by Jo Zarboulas..244

THE *Living* EARTH

written and illustrated by
Eleonore Schmid

Appreciative Listening

Appreciative listening is listening for
language that helps you create a picture
in your mind. Listen to the focus questions
your teacher will read to you.

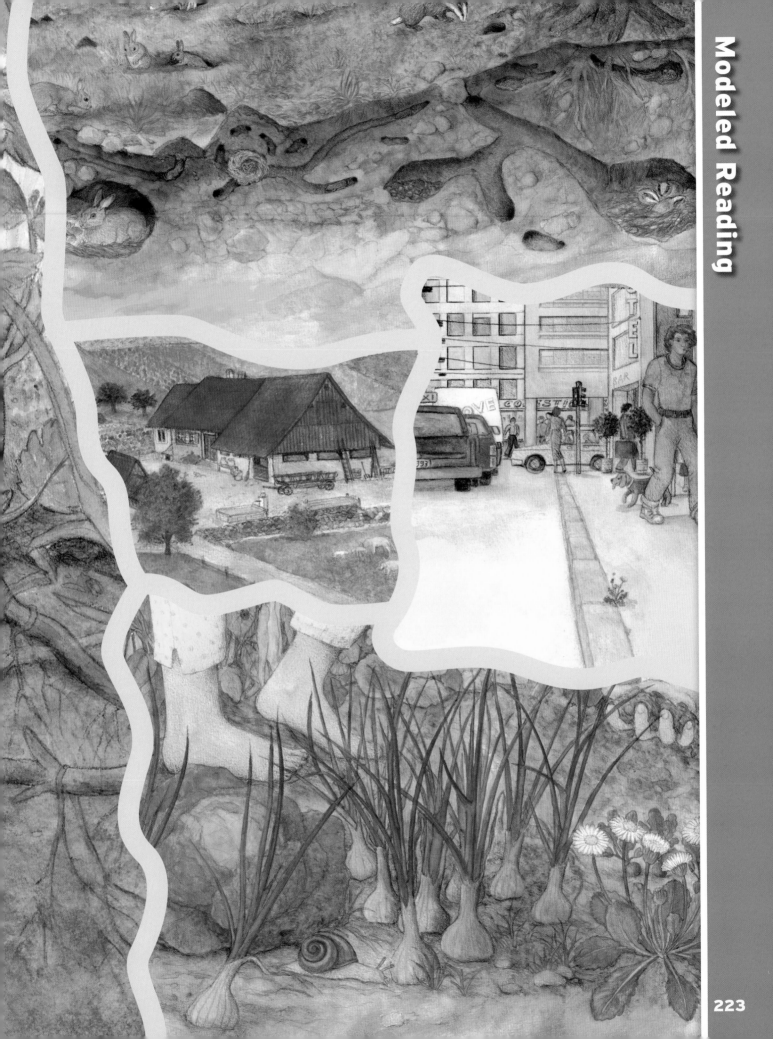

George Washington Carver

July 11

Dear Diary,

We visited the George Washington Carver National Monument today. I knew a few things about Mr. Carver already. I knew people called him the Plant Doctor. I learned that he made his own soil. Mr. Carver found that good potting soils **consist** of sand, fertile earth, and clay.

I also learned that Mr. Carver went to college at Iowa State. He studied plants and **geology**. I bet studying what's in each **layer** of earth helped him make better soil. I wonder what **property** of soil Mr. Carver thought was the most important.

I knew that Mr. Carver told southern farmers to plant peanuts. I didn't know that planting peanuts would help the soil. I learned that many farmers only planted cotton. This exhausted the soil. Planting peanuts put good things back in the soil. I guess Mr. Carver didn't want farmers to use **artificial** fertilizers to make the soil better.

Structured Vocabulary Discussion

Work with a small group to review all of your vocabulary words. Discuss in your group the vocabulary word that each of the following phrases suggest.

A single part of something piled up

The study of the Earth underground

Made up of

Throughout the week, add to your vocabulary journal entries. Record new insights and other words that relate to this week's vocabulary.

Picture It

Copy this word organizer into your vocabulary journal. Fill in each blank with something that is a **property** of soil.

property

color

_____

_____

_____

_____

Copy this word organizer into your vocabulary journal. Fill in the sections with things that can be **artificial**.

flowers

artificial

Ask Questions

Take time to ask questions as you read. Use your curiosity to improve your understanding. Asking your own questions keeps you thinking about your reading.

What QUESTIONS do you have about what you read?

Think about the questions you have in your mind as you read.

TURN AND TALK Listen to your teacher read the following lines from *The Living Earth*. Then, with a partner, discuss the questions you have and create your own questions about the passage.

• What things do you wonder about as you are reading?

• What questions can you ask while you are reading?

To get a bigger harvest, some farmers put artificial fertilizers in the soil. They spray the crops with chemicals, to kill the insects and diseases that attack the plants. And some farmers grow the same crops year after year after year.

This way of farming may produce bigger harvests, but it also hurts the land. The tiny organisms that live in the soil are harmed. Worms can't travel through the packed-down earth. The land is slowly drained of its nutrients, so more and more fertilizers are needed to produce new crops.

TAKE IT WITH YOU You will gain more from your reading if you create your own questions as you read. Try to ask question before, during, and after you read. As you read other selections, use a chart like the one below to help you create your own questions.

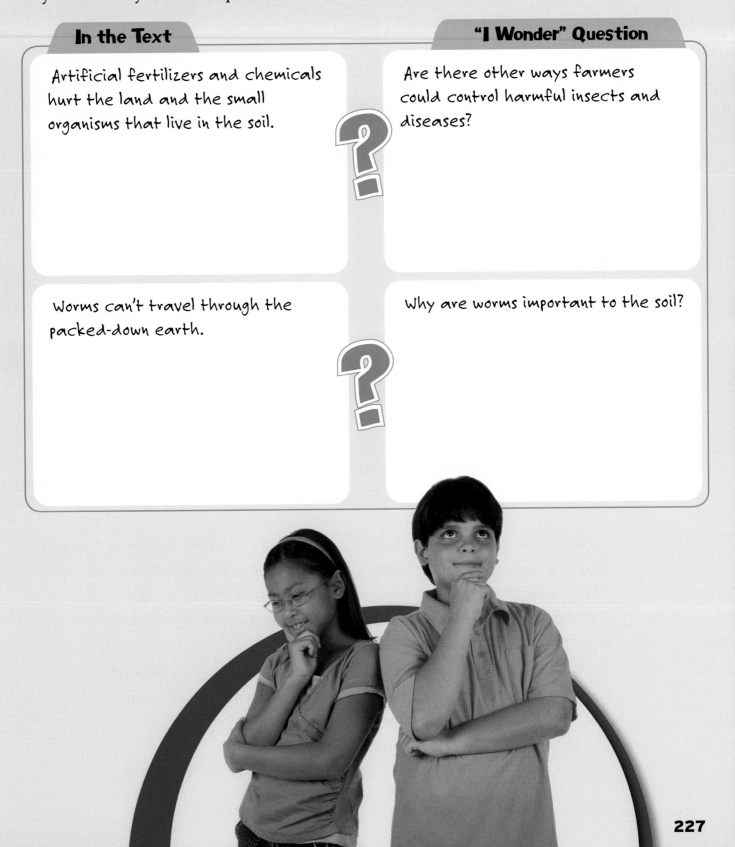

In the Text	"I Wonder" Question
Artificial fertilizers and chemicals hurt the land and the small organisms that live in the soil.	Are there other ways farmers could control harmful insects and diseases?
Worms can't travel through the packed-down earth.	Why are worms important to the soil?

A Very Dirty SUBJECT

by Karen Lowther

Carla wiped the sweat from her brow as she helped her mother plant their garden. "What an absolutely horrible Saturday!" she thought.

Carla sat mindlessly watching an earthworm burrow its way into the soil. Closing her eyes, she whispered, "I wish I could follow you into the cool soil and escape this dreadful work." As Carla repeated her wish for the third time, she felt her body slide below the dark, moist soil.

"It's lunchtime," said a voice. Carla jumped. The earthworm wriggled directly in front of her. "Feel free to snack on some soil, but I wouldn't recommend the rocks."

"What?" asked Carla in bewilderment.

"Oh, you're a first-timer, I can dig it," the worm chuckled. "Get it? 'Dig' it?"

Carla laughed. "Yeah, I get it," she said. "Thanks for letting me 'worm' my way out of lunch!"

"Hey, you're funny!" the worm chortled. "Now follow me—you've got a lot to learn about a very 'dirty' subject."

Carla tunneled her way after the worm, listening as it talked and munched its way through the soil. The worm knew a lot about soil. Suddenly the worm stopped and Carla bumped into it. A giant mole faced them, hungrily licking its lips. "I'm not ready to be somebody's supper—let's go!" cried the worm.

Carla shut her eyes tightly and said, "Give me sunshine and garden work." As she repeated her wish for the third time, Carla felt a hand on her shoulder.

"Are you feeling okay, dear? I said it's lunchtime," Carla's mom said, handing her a sandwich on a plate.

"Worms!" Carla panicked. Then she let out a nervous giggle—"No, just sprouts." Still, for a second, Carla was certain she spotted a sprout wiggling its way beneath the mustard.

Clay City STUDIO

OPEN DAILY 10 A.M. TO 9 P.M.

143 CLAY CITY ROAD

Come experience the rich tradition of pottery making. Our studio uses only the best clay. You'll find no course grains in our clay! Clay City clay is mined right here in the Ohio River Valley. Come see what our clay has to offer.

Why We Use Only Ohio Clay

Our local clay has fine particles. This makes the clay easy to work when wet. Ohio clay can be molded into beautiful shapes. The silky texture of the clay produces a strong, smooth surface. The finished piece has a firm texture that is just right for painting. Ohio clay is the perfect clay for creating valuable treasures!

Come join the fun. Whether you are an eager beginner or a serious artist, we have a place for you. Make one piece or make a hundred. Let Clay City Studio be your guide to the wonderful world of pottery!

Adjectives

About Adjectives

Adjectives are words that describe nouns or pronouns. Adjectives answer one of the three questions: What kind? How many? Which one? In the sentence "The wall has a rough texture," *rough* is an adjective that describes the noun *wall*. *Rough* answers the question "What kind of wall"? *Rough* describes how the wall feels. As your teacher reads the advertisement, listen for the adjectives.

Adjectives in Context

With a partner, read *Clay City Studio*. Enter each adjective you find in a chart like the one below. Sort the adjectives according to which question the adjective answers.

WHAT KIND?	HOW MANY?	WHICH ONE?
firm	one	this

Activity **Two**

Explore Words Together

table	flower
soil	house
streets	clay

The list on the right contains nouns. Write an adjective to describe each noun. Choose at least one adjective that answers each question: What kind? How many? Which one? Share what you wrote with a partner.

Activity **Three**

Explore Words in Writing

Choose three of the adjective/noun combinations you listed above. Write a sentence using each of the word pairs you chose. Share your favorite sentence with a partner.

THE CASE OF Vanishing Soil

by Darlene Stille

What Makes Soil Disappear?

I read recently that soil good enough for farming is disappearing up to 40 times faster than nature can replace it. My question is: What can we do about it? More importantly, what can I do about it?

I'm not a farmer, but I use soil to grow flowers in our backyard. This year, I'm planning to grow some vegetables.

So I decided to play soil detective. I asked myself some tough questions. I did some research. I tracked down two main culprits responsible for vanishing soil. Erosion is the worst culprit. Next in line is damaged soil.

What Is Erosion?

I learned that two kinds of erosion affect soil. Wind erosion blows the rich, top layer of soil away from farm fields. Water erosion washes good soil into lakes and rivers. Plowing farmland loosens soil and leads to water and wind erosion. Cutting down trees in forests destroys tree roots that hold soil in place. Cattle and sheep that eat all the grasses on prairies leave the soil totally unprotected.

What questions could you ask yourself to help you understand erosion?

Soil erosion

232

What Can Help Stop Erosion?

I can stop erosion in my own backyard. Our yard has plenty of trees and shrubs to protect against wind erosion, but water erosion is a problem. The land at the back of our garden slopes downhill. During a heavy spring rain, I watched muddy water run down from the garden. It dug out little ditches, called "rills," in the sloping soil. The little rills joined together to form bigger rills. In my research I read that rills can join to dig out a deep ditch called a "gully." Rushing rainwater carries good soil away through rills and gullies.

Farmers use a plan called "contour plowing" to help stop such water erosion. They plow ridges in the soil across a slope. The ridges trap water. Farmers in places with steep hills make big terraces for planting crops. Terraces look like steps around a hillside. Like the farmers, I can stop erosion in my sloping garden by building little terraces. I can plant flowers on the flat parts of my terrace steps.

How might you use the idea of contour plowing on a small scale in a garden?

Contour plowing

What Is Soil Damage?

Sometimes soil does not have the right kind of nutrients to grow flowers or vegetables. To help the plants grow, farmers usually add fertilizers. To control the pests that attack the plants, farmers might also use pesticides. Using the wrong kind of fertilizers or pesticides or too much of them may damage the soil.

I did a soil test on my backyard and found that my soil did not have the right kind of nutrients for growing tomatoes. I thought that I could fix my soil by just adding fertilizer. I did not want to damage my soil, so I had to do more research. I found that I could use either chemical fertilizer or natural fertilizer.

Chemical fertilizers are easy to use. I can buy bags of them at a store. However, I run the risk of hurting the water. These products can wash off the land into lakes and rivers after a rainstorm.

The things in fertilizer that help land plants grow also help water plants grow. Water plants clog rivers and block out sunlight. When the plants die, they become food for bacteria. Bacteria use up oxygen in the water that fish and other animals need.

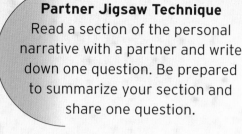

Partner Jigsaw Technique
Read a section of the personal narrative with a partner and write down one question. Be prepared to summarize your section and share one question.

How does chemical soil fertilizer add to the problem of water pollution?

Water plants clogging river

World Chemical Fertilizer Use
Fertilizer Use (in millions of metric tons)

Year	Fertilizer Use
1970/71	(69.15)
1975/76	(97.10)
1980/81	(117.20)
1985/86	(129.47)
1990/91	(138.24)
1995/96	(129.56)
2000/01	(135.56)

What Can Prevent Soil Damage?

I decided to use a natural fertilizer called *compost*. Compost creates fertile soil. It also will let me recycle my leftover coffee grounds, dead leaves, and torn up newspapers (brown materials). I can also recycle vegetables and grass clippings (green materials).

I started a compost pile in a corner of the yard. I used wooden stakes and wire mesh to make a fence. The fence made a container for my compost.

Making a good compost pile is a lot like making a layer cake. I put in layers of brown and green materials. I added a little soil between layers. When my pile grew to about three feet high, I mixed it up with a garden shovel. I kept churning and mixing as the brown and green layers began to combine. The center of the pile gets steamy hot! The process of decay gives off heat.

What questions do you have about compost?

Compost pile

What's Good About Erosion?

I read a surprising fact: Worms and insects also cause erosion—especially in the spring. After farmers plow their fields, soil creatures churn up and loosen the soil. If a big rain comes, whoosh! The water carries huge amounts of soil away from the fields. We need the animals that live in the soil. Their churning makes space in the soil to hold water and allow roots to grow. We need the farmers and their crops. These needs make the problem of vanishing soil very complex.

It turns out that we can't do away with erosion. Strange as it may seem, some erosion is actually good. Wind and water erode solid rock into smaller and smaller pieces. Dead plants and insects build up on the eroded rock to create rich humus. Together, the bits of rock and the humus form soil. Without erosion, we couldn't have soil at all!

Why is some erosion good?

A handful of earthworms

Think and Respond

Reflect and Write

- You and your partner read a section of *The Case of Vanishing Soil*. Discuss with your partner the questions you asked and their answers.

- On one side of an index card, write down one of the questions that you asked. On the other side, write down the answer that you and your partner discussed. Find another partner pair that read a different section and discuss with them your questions.

Adjectives in Context

Reread *The Case of Vanishing Soil* to find examples of adjectives. Write down the words you find. Then write three sentences about soil, using some of the adjectives from your list. Exchange your sentences with a partner. Circle the adjectives in the sentences and tell which question they answer: What kind? How many? Which one?

Turn and Talk

ASK QUESTIONS

Discuss with a partner what you have learned so far about how to ask questions.

- What does it mean to ask questions while you read?

- When and why should you ask questions about what you read?

Choose one of the questions you created about *The Case of Vanishing Soil*. Discuss with a partner why you asked the question and how you found the answer.

Critical Thinking

In a small group talk about how fertile soil is being lost to erosion and damage to the soil. Discuss why chemical fertilizers can be useful as well as harmful. On one side of a sheet of paper write a list of your ideas. Look back at *The Case of Vanishing Soil*. On the other side of the sheet of paper, write down ideas about soil erosion and damage to the soil from the article. Then discuss these questions.

- Why do many people use chemical fertilizers instead of compost?

- Why do other people use compost?

Making Compost

Compost is a fertile, dark soil. It is made from **particles** of decayed plant and animal waste. Compost helps plants grow. It can **replace** lost topsoil. Compost makes the **texture** of soil light and fluffy. Compost also helps soil hold water. Many gardeners make their own compost. You, too, can make compost by following this simple recipe.

Ingredients

brown materials, such as dried leaves, straw, and hay

green materials, such as grass clippings, weeds, and vegetable scraps or fruit peelings from the kitchen

soil or horse manure

water

STEP 1: Sort your compost materials into brown and green piles.

STEP 2: Make 6-inch layers of greens and browns. **Separate** each layer with 2 inches of soil or manure. Sprinkle each layer with water. Keep making layers until your pile is 3 to 5 feet high.

STEP 3: **Combine** the layers by stirring your pile every two weeks. A good compost pile will get hot inside. The pile will cook as if it were an oven.

STEP 4: Apply the compost to your garden and enjoy the rewards!

Structured Vocabulary Discussion

Work with a partner to complete the following sentences about your vocabulary words.

Separate and *combine* are *different* because . . .

Texture and *particles* are similar because . . .

Throughout the week, add to your vocabulary journal entries. Record new insights and other words that relate to this week's vocabulary.

Picture It

Copy this word organizer into your vocabulary journal. Fill in the sections with words that could describe a **texture** of something.

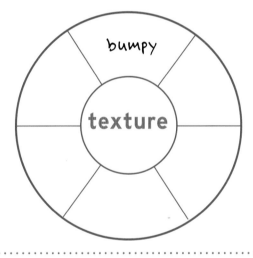

bumpy

texture

Copy this word organizer into your vocabulary journal. Fill in the circles with things that have **particles**.

compost

particles

What Does Weather Do to Soil?

by Ann Weil

Soil
lovely loam
clingy clay
humid humus

Rain pours down
rip-roaring rain
soft soupy soil
slippery sloppy soil

Sun shines down
hot rocks swell
icy night air chills the ground
cold rocks shrink
hot cold hot cold
swell shrink swell shrink
crack crash
rocks break apart and
separate into smaller bits

Gusts blow
across the gravelly ground
whipping dirt into storms
turbulent soil rides the wind

LANDSLIDE!

April 12, 2007

Dear Zach,

You'll never guess what I saw yesterday—a landslide! It was unbelievable! I was hiking with my family not far from home. Other than being awfully muddy, nothing seemed unusual.

All of a sudden, we heard a loud noise. Dad said it sounded like trees cracking. It made me uncomfortable because I didn't know where it came from. Then we saw the problem on a nearby mountain. There were trees falling—lots of them!

We felt the ground shaking, and I started shaking too. That's how uneasy I felt. Dad shouted, "Landslide!" He pointed to red mud and rocks sliding down the side of the other mountain. More trees cracked and boulders banged together. Even though it was far away, it sounded so loud!

I felt terrible because I was unable to stop it. All we could do was watch. Luckily, there were no houses below the landslide. That would have been awful. Still, the whole thing was so unexpected it shook me up. Hopefully, I won't ever see another landslide!

Mark

Landslide!

Prefix *un-*

Activity One

About the Prefix *un-*

A prefix is a letter or group of letters that is added to the beginning of a word to change that word's meaning. The prefix *un-* means *not*. For example, the word *usual* means "common." The word *unusual* means "not common." As your teacher reads Mark's letter, listen for the words that have the prefix *un-*.

Prefix *un-* in Context

With a partner, read the letter. Find as many *un-* words as you can and place them in a chart like the one below. Then write the meaning of each word, its root word, and the meaning of the root word.

UN- WORD	MEANING	ROOT WORD	MEANING
unable	cannot do	able	can do

Activity Two

Explore Words Together

The list on the right contains six words. Work with a partner to add the prefix *un-* to each of the words. Then together, think of two additional *un-* words for your list. Explain the meanings of each *un-* word and its root.

friendly   married
lock   afraid
fold   broken

Activity Three

Explore Words in Writing

Write an *un-* story. Create a story using the *un-* words you made above plus as many other *un-* words as you can. Have fun with it! Share your *un-* story with a partner.

THE BLACK BLIZZARD

by Jo Zarboulas

"Can history repeat itself?" Sam wondered anxiously. "Could the Black Blizzard come back?"

Sam was milking the cow in the barn. He began thinking about the Black Blizzard when he looked out the open barn door and saw a huge, black cloud gathering. It didn't look like an ordinary rain cloud. Besides, there hadn't been any clouds for along time. There was a drought here in the Oklahoma panhandle.

Since he had been a toddler, Sam had heard about the Black Blizzard. Years ago, it had caused many families to abandon their farms and move away. At first, Sam thought it was a monstrous animal, like a giant black buzzard, that ate all the wheat and vegetables on the farm. Later, he understood more. The Black Blizzard was monstrous, all right, but it wasn't an animal. It was a huge dust storm.

Now as Sam watched the dark cloud roll in, he was worried. Perhaps this cloud, or one like it, would grow into a Black Blizzard.

> Why would a duststorm be called the Black Blizzard?

Sam thought of questions to ask Gramps, his great-grandfather. Gramps had been in the first Black Blizzard when he was Sam's age. Sam's questions would have to wait, though; Gramps and Sam's mother were in town.

"Meanwhile, I'll think of the story that Gramps tells," Sam said to himself. He closed his eyes and could almost hear Gramps's voice.

Who is telling the story about the Black Blizzard?

It hadn't rained for a long time. The wheat in the fields was withering, the tomatoes in the garden were as small as stones, and the lima beans weren't worth eating. There wasn't much left to eat. Mostly we ate vegetables that Ma had put up in Mason jars the year before and eggs from our chickens.

April 14th, 1935, was a day I'll never forget. I was in the fields helping Pa clear out the dead wheat. Suddenly we saw huge black clouds billowing up. The clouds started coming at us, fast as a locomotive. "Run!" Pa shouted with alarm. We ran frantically in the direction of the house, which we could barely see in the sudden darkness.

In the farmhouse, Ma, Pa, and I feverishly stuffed cloths under the doors and windows to keep out the dust. Then we huddled together, listening to the wind howl.

When the storm was over, dirt was piled to the windowsills and two feet of dirt blocked the front door. Pa had to climb out a window to shovel it away. After that, we lived in fear that the Black Blizzard would return—and it did, many times. We had to get used to those huge black clouds and all the destruction they brought. The Black Blizzard became a frequent, unwelcome, and unavoidable visitor.

When we had to go out, the dust stung our eyes. We wore bandanas over our faces, but dust still filled our nostrils and choked our lungs. When we ate, we swallowed mouthfuls of dust. Ma cleaned and swept, trying to keep ahead of the dust. Pa kept plowing and planting, driving the tractor almost blind from the dust in his eyes and the darkness that surrounded him.

Why was the dust an unwelcome visitor?

Their hard work was in vain, though. The dust kept coming, and there was no wheat to sell that year. Later, things got even worse. One night I heard Ma and Pa talking when they thought I was asleep. Ma said the Dales, our neighbors, were going to leave their farm and move to California to find work. Pa said maybe we'd have to do that, too.

Sam heard the truck driving up. Mom and Gramps were home! Sam ran to greet them. "Gramps, I want to ask you some questions about the Black Blizzard," he said urgently.

"Sure, Sam. Let's sit here," Gramps replied.

Sam ran his finger over the table. "Look at this dust, Gramps. It has a soft texture, and if I look closely, I can see it's made of tiny particles. How can something so soft and tiny ruin crops and cause people to abandon their farms?"

Well," said Gramps, "in this area, dust is actually soil from the fields. Topsoil—the top layer of soil—contains nutrition that crops need. Topsoil to crops is like food to us. In a drought, wind blows the topsoil away. Crops can't survive long without topsoil; animals and people can't survive long without crops."

"That makes sense," Sam said. "But why did so much topsoil blow away in the 1930s? I've experienced a few droughts, but so far, I've never seen a Black Blizzard."

How did farmers contribute to the Black Blizzard?

"Farmers back then contributed to the erosion problem," replied Gramps. "They made lots of money selling wheat, so they plowed under vast amounts of grasslands to plant additional crops. The grasslands had anchored the topsoil, which helped prevent erosion; the wheat fields left the topsoil exposed. After a long drought, the winds gathered up the bare topsoil into tremendous clouds of dust— the Black Blizzard."

Just then, there was a loud rumbling noise. Sam ran to the window, his heart pounding. "Oh, no! The Black Blizzard has returned!" he thought anxiously. Then he heard a familiar noise on the roof. Rain, glorious rain!

What does Sam think is happening when he first hears the rumbling sound?

Sam, Mom, and Gramps watched with relief from the window as the rain poured down. Then Sam said, "Gramps, I have one more question. Could it happen again? Could a Black Blizzard return and ruin us—force us to abandon our farm?"

"Well, Sam," Gramps replied thoughtfully, "droughts have come to the panhandle of Oklahoma for centuries, and they'll come again. But the government and farmers know more now about protecting the topsoil and stopping erosion. They work hard to keep Black Blizzards from returning. Assuming you stay on the farm, you'll help, too, Sam," Gramps said. "You'll learn about farming methods that protect the soil, and you'll do everything you can to preserve it."

"Yes, Gramps, I will," Sam said, nodding his head. "As you say, 'If we take care of the land, it will take care of us.'"

Think and Respond

Reflect and Write

- You and your partner took turns retelling *The Black Blizzard*. Discuss any parts you had trouble understanding, and what you did to help make things clearer.

- Choose two parts of the story that were hardest for you to understand. On one side of an index card, write a word, sentence, or part of the story that you had trouble understanding. On the back of the card, write what you did to make the meaning more clear.

Prefix *-un* in Context

Reread *The Black Blizzard* to find examples of words that could have the prefix *-un* added to them. List each word. Compare your list with the list of a partner. Then pick five words from each list and provide definitions. Share your words and definitions with the class.

Turn and Talk
MONITOR UNDERSTANDING

Discuss with a partner what you have learned so far about monitoring understanding while you read.

- How do you monitor understanding?

- Why is it important to monitor understanding?

Reread *The Black Blizzard*. Then reread the descriptions you and a partner created for the Reflect and Write activity. Discuss whether any of the descriptions need revision. If needed, revise your descriptions.

Critical Thinking

With a small group, brainstorm what you know about the properties of soil. Write your ideas down in a list. Then look back over *The Black Blizzard*. Discuss what the Black Blizzard was and how farmers helped cause the Black Blizzard. Then write answers to these questions.

- How do farmers today try to avoid creating dust storms?

- How does the information on the Black Blizzard fit with what you already know about soil?

Glossary

Using the Glossary

Like a dictionary, this glossary lists words in alphabetical order. Guide words at the top of each page show you the first and last word on the page. If a word has more than one syllable, the syllables are separated by a dark dot (•). Use the pronunciation key on the bottom of page 251.

Sample

The pronunciation guide shows how to say the word. The accent shows which syllable is stressed.

The part of speech shows how the word is often used.

Each word is broken into syllables.

con•ser•va•tory (kən sur′ və tôr′ ē) *n.* A glass room for growing and showing plants. *The conservatory was filled with plants from around the world.*

The definition shows what the word means.

The example sentence includes the word in it.

Abbreviations: *adj.* adjective, *adv.* adverb, *conj.* conjunction, *interj.* interjection, *n.* noun, *prep.* preposition, *pron.* pronoun, *v.* verb

---

aisle • conservatory

aisle (īl) *n.* A passageway between rows of something, such as seats, shelves, or counters. *The aisle between the counters was crowded with shoppers.*

a•quar•i•um (ə kwer′ ē əm) *n.* A glass tank or bowl in which water animals and plants are kept. *I counted ten brightly colored fish in the aquarium.*

back•bone (bak′ bōn′) *n.* The column of bones along the center of the back in humans, dogs, cats, and other vertebrate animals. *A snake's backbone is long.*

blight (blīt) *n.* A condition or disease that kills plants or hurts their growth. *The potato blight wiped out the entire crop.*

bo•tan•ic (bə tan′ ik) *adj.* Of or about plants. *The botanic garden had many plants.*

cam•ou•flage (kam′ ə fläzh′) *v.* **camouflaged** Hidden by making something look like its surroundings. *The lizard's green skin camouflaged its presence in the garden.*

cap•sule (kap′ səl) *n.* A container. *The space capsule, with the astronauts inside, landed safely in the ocean.*

car•niv•o•rous (kär niv′ ə rəs) *adj.* Meat-eating. *Lions and tigers are carnivorous animals.*

con•ser•va•tory (kən sur′ və tory) *n.* A glass room for growing and showing plants. *The conservatory was filled with plants from around the world.*

con·tour (kän´ tōōr´) *adj.* Made to follow the shape or outline of something. ***Contour*** *plowing helps farmers prevent soil erosion.*

cramped (krampt) *adj.* Small or crowded. *The family lived in* ***cramped*** *rooms.*

cul·prit (kul´ prit) *n.* Someone who has done something wrong. *When my mother found the spilt milk, she thought my brother was the likely* ***culprit.***

deli·cate (del´ i kit) *adj.* Easily damaged. *The sand dollar was very* ***delicate.***

diph·ther·i·a (dif thir´ ē ə) *n.* A disease that causes high fever, coughing, and trouble breathing. *The townspeople were worried that many people would catch* ***diphtheria.***

eth·nic (eth´ nik) *adj.* Of or about people who share a common national background. *Many people enjoy* ***ethnic*** *foods and music.*

ex·haust (eg zôst´) *v.* **exhausted** To use up or wear out. *The farmers* ***exhausted*** *the soil by always planting the same crop.*

fluid (flōō´ id) *n.* Water or other liquid that can flow easily. *The* ***fluid*** *spilled from the broken bottle.*

fluo·res·cent (flô res´ ənt) *adj.* Glowing or very bright. *The shirt was a bright* ***fluorescent*** *orange.*

frail (frāl) *adj.* Weak and slender. *The sick boy was very* ***frail.***

her·it·age (her´ ə tij) *n.* Something handed down from a person's ancestors or past. *Celebrating the Fourth of July is part of our nation's* ***heritage.***

labo·ra·tory (lab´ rə tôr´ ē) *n.* A room or building where scientists perform experiments or tests. *The two scientists shared the* ***laboratory.***

mon·strous (män´ strəs) *adj.* Large or huge. *The* ***monstrous*** *wave washed over the ship.*

mon·u·ment (män´ yōō mənt) *n.* Something built or created to keep alive the memory of a person or event. *We visited George Washington's* ***monument*** *in Washington, D.C.*

nu·tri·tion (nōō trish´ ən) *n.* Food. *Good* ***nutrition*** *and exercise help keep people healthy.*

quail (kwāl) *n.* A small, short-tailed bird. *We saw a* ***quail*** *looking for food.*

PRONUNCIATION KEY		
a add, map	oi oil, boy	zh vision, pleasure
ā ace, rate	ou pout, now	ə the schwa, an
â(r) care, air	ōō took, full	unstressed vowel
ä palm, father	ōō pool, food	representing the
e end, pet	u up, done	sound spelled
ē equal, tree	ŧ care, her,	*a* in *above*
i it, give	sir, burn,	*e* in *sicken*
ī ice, write	word	*i* in *possible*
o odd, hot	yōō fuse, few	*o* in *melon*
ō open, so	z zest, wise	*u* in *circus*
ô order, jaw		

reef (rēf) *n.* A ridge of coral, rock, or sand near the surface of the water. *The coral **reef** was home to many fish.*

rem·e·dy (rem′ ə dē) *v.* To correct, heal, or put right. *I tried to **remedy** the problem by turning off the water.*

re·veal (ri vēl′) *v.* To make known. *My teacher did not **reveal** the ending of the book.*

salsa (säl′ sə) *n.* A type of Latin American dance music. *I really like **salsa** music because of its rhythm.*

sed·i·ment (sed′ ə mənt) *n.* 1. Any material that settles to the bottom of a liquid. 2. Stone and earth carried by wind and water. *After the flood, **sediment** covered the road.*

seg·ment·ed (seg′ ment əd) *adj.* Divided into parts or pieces. *The worm's body had a **segmented** look.*

skel·e·ton (skel′ ə tən) *n.* The framework of bones inside an animal's body. *I found the **skeleton** of a fish on the beach.*

snor·kel·ing (snôr′ kəl ing) *v.* To move or swim underwater using a breathing tube. *I was **snorkeling** in Key West.*

snug (snug) *adj.* Warm and cozy. *I love my **snug** little house.*

spe·cif·ic (spə sif′ ik) *adj.* Particular or special kind. *I wanted a **specific** type of red apple.*

sta·lac·tites (stə lak′ tīts) *n.* Cone-shaped mineral deposits that hang from the roof of a cave. *The **stalactites** looked like giant icicles inside the cave.*

sta·lag·mites (stə lag′ mīts) *n.* Cone-shaped mineral deposits that build up from the floor of a cave. *We walked between the **stalagmites** in the cave.*

sum·mit (sum′ it) *n.* The highest point or part; the top. *We reached the **summit** of the mountain at noon.*

ter·rar·i·um (tə rer′ ē əm) *n.* A glass container in which small plants and animals are kept. *My job was to feed the animals in the **terrarium**.*

traits (trāts) *n.* Qualities or characteristics. *Having eight legs is one of the **traits** that spiders share.*

trough (trôf) *n.* A long, narrow container for holding water or food. *The cattle drank water from the **trough**.*

ty·phoon (tī fōōn′) *n.* A violent storm with high winds; the name for a hurricane in the western Pacific Ocean. *The people were glad the **typhoon** missed their island.*

u·nique (yōō nēk′) *adj.* The only one of its kind. *The dance was **unique**.*

veg·e·tar·ian (vej′ ə ter′ ē ən) *n.* A person who eats vegetables but does not eat meat. *My aunt is a **vegetarian**.*

webbed (webd) *adj.* Joined like a web. *Ducks have **webbed** feet.*

weird (wird) *adj.* Strange. *The web-footed dog was very **weird**.*

Cover Acknowledgements

For permission to reprint copyrighted material, grateful acknowledgment is made to the following sources:

Boyd Mills Press, Inc. A Highlights Company 815 Church Street, Honesdale, Pennsylvania 18431: from *A Century Farm* by Cris Peterson. Text ©1999. Photographs by Alvis Upitis ©1999.

Candlewick Press: from *Seal* by Judy Allen, illustrated by Tudor Humphries. Text ©1993. Illustrations ©1993.

Dutton Children's Books, a division of Penguin Putnam Books for Young Readers: from *Oranges on Golden Mountain*, by Elizabeth Partridge, illustrated by Aki Sogabe Text ©2001. Illustrations ©2001.

Groundwood Books/House of Anansi press 720 Bathurst St. Suite 500, Toronto, Ontario M5S 2R4: from *Very Last First Time* by Jan Andrews, illustrated by Ian Wallace, 2005. Text ©1985. Illustrations © 1985.

Katherine Tegen Books, an Imprint of Harper Collins: from *Firestorm* by Jean Craighead George. Illustrated by Wendell Minor. Text ©2003. Illustrations ©2003.

North-South Books, an imprint of Nord-Süd Verlag AG, Gossau Zürich, Switzerland: from *The Living Earth* by Elenore Schmid. Illustrated by Elenore Schmid. ©1994.

Scholatstic Inc.: from *Coming to America: The Story of Immigration* by Betsy Maestro, illustrated by Susannah Ryan. Text ©1996. Illustrations ©1996.

Walker Publishing Co.: from *Arctic Nights, Arctic Lights* by Debbie S. Miller. Illustrated by Jon Van Zyle. Text ©2003. Illustrations ©2003.

Unit Opener Acknowledgements

P.2a ©David David Gallery, Philidelphia, Pennsylvania, USA; p.64a ©Christie's Image/CORBIS; p.126a ©Muskegon Museum of Art; p.188a ©SuperStock, Inc./SuperStock

Illustration Acknowledgements

P.12a, TSP1 Burgandy Beam/Wilkinson Studios; p.13b, TSP2 Burgandy Beam/Wilkinson Studios; p.14a, b Micha Archer/Wilkinson Studios; p.16a Luanne Marten/Wilkinson Studios; p.18a Luanne Marten/Wilkinson Studios; p.20a Luanne Marten/Wilkinson Studios; p.21a Luanne Marten/Wilkinson Studios; p.22a Luanne Marten/Wilkinson Studios; p.24a Drew Rose/Wilkinson Studios; p.28a, b Ron Mahoney/Wilkinson Studios; p.30a Ron Mahoney/Wilkinson Studios; p.32a, b Ron Mahoney/Wilkinson Studios; p.33a Ron Mahoney/Wilkinson Studios; p.42a George Hamblin/Wilkinson Studios; p.43c George Hamblin/Wilkinson Studios; p.44 b, c Gary Krejca/Wilkinson Studios; p.52a Chris Pappas/Wilkinson Studios; p.54a Diana Kizlauskas/Wilkinson Studios; p.58a Kevin Serwacki/Wilkinson Studios; p.60a Kevin Serwacki/Wilkinson Studios; p.62a Kevin Serwacki/Wilkinson Studios; p.63a Kevin Serwacki/Wilkinson Studios; p.70a Dennis Franzen/Wilkinson Studios; p.71a Dennis Franzen/Wilkinson Studios; p.75d Jonathan Massie/Wilkinson Studios; p.78a Stan Gorman/Wilkinson Studios; p.80a Stan Gorman/Wilkinson Studios; p.82a Stan Gorman/Wilkinson Studios; p.92d Jared Osterhold/Wilkinson Studios; p.94d Jared Osterhold/Wilkinson Studios; p.100b, c Ralph Canaday/Wilkinson Studios; p.104a Francesca Carabelli/Wilkinson Studios; p.105a Francesca Carabelli/Wilkinson Studios; p.108 a, b Dean Lindberg/Wilkinson Studios; p.109b, c Dean Lindberg/Wilkinson Studios; p.110b Dean Lindberg/Wilkinson Studios; p.111b, c Dean Lindberg/Wilkinson Studios; p.112c Dean Lindberg/Wilkinson Studios; p.120a Micha Archer/Wilkinson Studios; p.122a Micha Archer/Wilkinson Studios; p.124b Micha Archer/Wilkinson Studios; p.140a Brad Teare/Wilkinson Studios; p.142a Brad Teare/Wilkinson Studios; p.144a Brad Teare/Wilkinson Studios; p.145a Brad Teare/Wilkinson Studios; p.148a Julia Woolf/Wilkinson Studios; p.152a, b, c, d Tom Katsulis/Wilkinson Studios; p.153b, c Tom Katsulis/Wilkinson Studios; p.154a, b, c Tom Katsulis/Wilkinson Studios; p.155b, c Tom Katsulis/Wilkinson Studios; p.156a, b, c Tom Katsulis/Wilkinson Studios; p.170a, b Vicki Bradley/Wilkinson Studios; p.172a, b Vicki Bradley/Wilkinson Studios; p.173b Vicki Bradley/Wilkinson Studios; p.174a, b, c Vicki Bradley/Wilkinson Studios; p.199a Jonathan Massie/Wilkinson Studios; p.200a, b Jonathan Massie/Wilkinson Studios; p.202a Pascale Constantin/Wilkinson Studios; p.204a Pascale Constantin/Wilkinson Studios; p.206a Pascale Constantin/Wilkinson Studios; p.210a Paula Zinngrabe-Wendland/Wilkinson Studios; p.212a Jonathan Massie/Wilkinson Studios; p.215c Jonathan Massie/Wilkinson Studios; p.216b Jonathan Massie/Wilkinson Studios; p.228a, b Reggie Holladay/Wilkinson Studios; p.229a, b Reggie Holladay/Wilkinson Studios; p.232c Dan Grant/Wilkinson Studios; p.240a Joe Boddy/Wilkinson Studios; p.241a Joe Boddy/Wilkinson Studios; p.244a Tom McNeely/Wilkinson Studios; p.246a Tom McNeely/Wilkinson Studios; p.248a Tom McNeely/Wilkinson Studios; p.249a Tom McNeely/Wilkinson Studios.

Photography Acknowledgements

P.4c ©Bettmann/Corbis; p.8a Frank Balthis; p.8b ©photocuisine/Corbis; p.9c ©Frank Balthis; p.12b ©Dinodia; p.14c ©Tim Hill/Stockfood America; p.15a ©Lisa Romerein/Jupiterimages; p.26a Element Photo Shoot; p.26b ©Herbert Spichtinger/zefa/Corbis; p.26c ©Hulton Archive/Getty Images; p.27b ©Hulton Archive/Getty Images; p.34a ©Larry Dale Gordon/Getty Images; p.34b ©Hubert Stadler/Corbis; p.38a ©Jeff Greenberg/Alamy; p.38b ©Philip Gould/Corbis; p.38c ©Wisser Bill/Corbis Sygma; p.39b Element Photo Shoot; p.42b, TSP 7, ©Werner Forman Archive/Central History Museum, P/Yongyang North Korea; p.43b Element Photo Shoot; p.43a,TSP 8, ©Pat Behnke/Alamy; p.44a Element Photo Shoot; p.45a ©Walter Cimbal/Stockfood Creative/Getty Images; p.46a,b Element Photo Shoot; p.46c ©Burke/Triolo Productions/Jupiterimages; p.46d ©Paul Poplis/Jupiterimages; p.47a Element Photo Shoot; p.47b ©William Lingwood/Stockfood Munich/Stockfood America; p.47c ©Renee Comet Photography, Inc./Stockfood America; p.47c ©Burke/Triolo Productions/Jupiterimages; p.47d ©Scott Payne/PictureQuest; p.48a,b Element Photo Shoot; p.48b ©Burke/Triolo Productions/Jupiterimages; p.48d ©Scott Payne/PictureQuest; p.49b Element Photo Shoot; p.49b ©Michael Rosenfeld/Getty Images; p.49c ©John Burwell/Jupiterimages; p.50a,b,c Element Photo Shoot; p.50a ©Rob Fiocca/Jupiterimages; p.50b ©Eric Futran/PictureQuest; p.50c ©Eisenhut and Mayer/PictureQuest; p.51a ©Burke/Triolo/PictureQuest; p.52b ©Jeff Greenberg/The Image Works; p.56a Element Photo Shoot; p.56b ©Martin Alipaz/epa/Corbis; p.56c ©Keren Su/Photographer's Choice/Getty Images; p.57a ©Kevin Fleming/Corbis; p.74a, TSP 13, ©Art Wolfe/Photo Researchers, Inc.; p.74b, TSP 13, ©Terry Whittaker/Photo Researchers, Inc.; p.74b,c, TSP 13, ©Karp, Darek/Animals Animals - Earth Scenes; p.75a, TSP 14, ©Art Wolfe/Photo Researchers, Inc.; p.75a,b, TSP 14, ©Gallo Images/Daryl Balfour/Getty Images; p.75b, TSP 14, ©Francois Gohier/Photo Researchers, Inc.; p.75c, TSP 14, ©William Grenfell/Visuals Unlimited; p.75c, TSP 14, ©Michael & Patricia Fogden/Minden Pictures; p.76a Element Photo Shoot; p.76b ©Terje Rakke/Getty Images; p.77a ©Stuart Westmorland/Getty Images; p.84a ©Alan Schein/zefa/Corbis; p.84b ©David Young-Wolff/Photo Edit; p.84c ©M. D. Madhusudan; p.85a ©M. D. Madhusudan; p.86a,b ©Frank Greenaway/Dorling Kindersley/Getty Images; p.86c ©Tom McHugh/Photo Researchers, Inc.; p.87a ©Louise Murray/Alamy; p.87b ©Ken Lucas/Visuals Unlimited; p.88b Element Photo Shoot; p.88a ©Mark Bolton/Corbis; p.88c ©Steve Bloom Images/Alamy; p.89a ©Katherine Feng/GLOBIO/Minden Pictures; p.90a Element Photo Shoot; p.90c ©Frans Lanting/Corbis; p.90d ©William Whitehurst/Corbis; p.91a ©Johner/Getty Images; p.91a ©Charles Krebs/Getty Images; p.92a Element Photo Shoot; p.92b ©Mark Moffett/Minden Pictures; p.92b ©Westend61/Alamy; p.92c ©Flip Nicklin/Minden Pictures; p.93a ©Photo Resource Hawaii/Alamy; p.93c ©Renee Lynn/Corbis; p.93d ©Doug Perrine/naturepl.com; p.94a Element Photo Shoot; p.94b ©Nature's Images/Photo Researchers, Inc.; p.94b ©Burke/Triole Producti/www.agefotostock.com; p.95a ©Karl H. Switak/Photo Researchers, Inc.; p.100a Element Photo Shoot; p.106b Element Photo Shoot; p.106c ©Bob Rowan; Progressive Image/Corbis; p.108a Element Photo Shoot; p.109d Element Photo Shoot; p.110a,c Element Photo Shoot; p.112a,b Element Photo Shoot; p.114b ©Robert J. Erwin/Photo Researchers; p.114c ©Stuart Wilson/Photo Researchers; p.115b ©Stephen P. Parker/Photo Researchers; p.132b ©Don Mason/Corbis; p.132c ©Scott T. Smith/AGPix; p.133b ©Konrad Wothe/Minden Pictures; p.136a, TSP 25, ©Allen Prier/Panoramic Images/NGSImages.com; p.138a Element Photo Shoot; p.138a ©David Muench/Corbis; p.138b ©David Lee Thompson; p.138c ©Danny Lehman/Corbis; p.138c ©Robert Landau/Corbis; p.138d ©Nic Cleave Photography/Alamy; p.139a ©David Muench/Corbis; p.146 a Element Photo Shoot; p.146b ©Erin Paul Donovan/Alamy; p.146c ©David Lyons/Alamy; p.146d ©David Muench/Corbis; p.147b ©Farrell Grehan/Corbis; p.150a Element Photo Shoot; p.150b ©Michael Snell/Alamy; p.150c ©James L. Amos/Corbis; p.152d ©Geoffrey Clifford/Getty Images; p.153c ©Images.com/Corbis; p.154c ©Philip Schermeister/Getty Images; p.155b ©Ron Watts/Corbis; p.156c ©Mark Wilson /SuperStock; p.158b ©Cameron Davidson/Alamy; p.158b ©Chris Trotman/Duomo/Corbis; p.162a ©photocuisine/Corbis; p.162b ©Associated Press, AP; p.162c ©Michael Rosenfeld/Getty Images; p.163a ©Simone Metz/Getty Images; p.163b ©Alaskastock; p.166b, TSP 31, ©Cameron Davidson/Alamy; p.167a, TSP 32, ©Susan and Neil Silverman; p.168c ©Gary Meszaros/Photo Researchers; p.169a ©Dave Bartruff/Corbis; p.175b ©Lake County Museum/Corbis; p.176a Element Photo Shoot; p.176b ©Steve Satushek/Getty Images; p.176c ©Darrell Gulin/Corbis; p.177a ©Dennis Frates/Alamy; p.178b Element Photo Shoot; p.178a ©Maps.com/Index Stock; p.178c ©Buddy Mays/Corbis; p.178d ©Win McNamee/Getty Images; p.179a Element Photo Shoot; p.179b ©Associated Press/Florida Keys News Bureau; p.179c ©Carl & Ann Purcell/Corbis; p.180a ©Andre Jenny/Alamy; p.180b ©Mike Powell/Getty Images; p.181a ©Associated Press/AP; p.182a ©Craig Tuttle/Corbis; p.182b ©PEMCO - Webster & Stevens Collection; Museum of History and Industry, Seattle/Corbis; p.183a ©Corbis; p.184a ©Bob Krist/Corbis; p.184b ©Lake County Museum/Corbis; p.186a Courtesy of the Northwest Museum of Arts & Culture/EWSHS; p.187a ©Associated Press/Cumberland; p.190b ©Tom Payne/Alamy; p.194a Element Photo Shoot; p.194b ©Bryan and Cherry Alexander Photography/Alamy; p.194c ©Burgess Blevins/Getty Images; p.195a ©Galen Rowell/Corbis; p.195b ©Werner Forman Archive/Canadian Museum of Civilization Location: 21 ©Werner Foreman/Topham/The Image Works; p.198a Element Photo Shoot; p.201a ©Kevin P. Casey/Corbis; p.201b ©Warren Bolster/Getty Images; p.208a ©Denny Eilers/Grant Heilman Photography; p.209a ©PicturePress/Getty Images; p.210b Element Photo Shoot; p.211b Element Photo Shoot; p.212b,c ©Norbert Wu/Peter Arnold, Inc.; p.212d ©Warren Bolster/Getty Images; p.213a ©Andrez/Getty Images; p.214a ©Kurt Scholz/SuperStock; p.215b ©Shepard Sherbell/Corbis; p.216a ©Sally A. Morgan; Ecoscene/Corbis; p.217b Element Photo Shoot; p.218a ©Murray, Patti/ Animals Animals/ Earth Scenes; p.219a ©Michael Melford/Getty Images; p.224a,b,d Element Photo Shoot; p.224d ©Hulton Archive/Getty Images; p.230a Element Photo Shoot; p.231a ©Francis G. Mayer/Corbis; p.232a,b Element Photo Shoot; p.232d ©Richard A. Cooke/Corbis; p.233c ©Mark Godfrey/The Image Works; p.234a,b Element Photo Shoot; p.234c ©NHPA/John Shaw; p.235c ©Oliver Strewe/Getty Images; p.236a,b Element Photo Shoot; p.236c ©Macduff Everton/Corbis; p.237a ©B. Runk/S. Schoenberger/Grant Heilman Photography; p.238a,b Element Photo Shoot; p.238c ©Chris Whitehead/Getty Images; p.239a ©Dorling Kindersly; p.242a,b,c Element Photo Shoot; p.242d ©Chuck Place/Alamy; p.243a ©Eastcott Momatiuk/Getty Images.

Additional photography by Alamy/Royalty Free; Comstock/Royalty Free; Corbis/Harcourt Index; Corbis/Royalty Free; Corbis/Royalty Free; Digital Vision/Harcourt Index; Dreamstime/Royalty Free; Eyewire/Getty Images Royalty Free; Getty Images/Royalty Free; PhotoDisc/Royalty Free; Royalty Free/Dreamstime.com; SuperStock/Royalty Free; Tongro Image Stock/Royalty Free.